THE OBITUARY

THE OBITUARY

Gail Scott

NIGHTBOAT BOOKS
CALLICOON, NEW YORK

for Anna

What haunts are not the dead but the gaps
left within us by the secrets of others.

—Abraham + Torok

R, NEGATIVE

Standing by a pond. Obsidian eyes turning this way +
that. Catching the amber lights of the pond's fractal
surface. Raising hands out at hips, palms down, throwing
legs out sideways from the knees, tossing head left +
back, Rose,+ her dissociates do a little dance. To the
grammar of the birds. Singing by the hundreds. Then
Grandpa's there beside her. He says this marsh will be
drained. He says the many will stop coming. He says
this is natural. The lord helps them who help themselves.

These Wars on the Radio
Are Keeping Us from Our Own

In pale Mile-End, behind the night sheds, little pink clouds come tippling tippling down. And huge yellow maple leaves, not cold enough to turn red, tumbling, tumbling on regrowing November grass, to lie like yellow hands. From the kitchen radio, the ack-ack-swat of the most sophisticated of bombs weighing up to two tons from the most fantastically shaped planes cut out of futuristic novels falling on rubbles of sand + broken stone desert people called home..........Oh X

do you remember
when Afghan spelt dope
embroidered vests, vast
windswept steppes
with tanned shaggy fashion models
standing slant on them?

*

I'm that Face on the 3rd. She looks out, barely visible behind those grey venetians in upper Triplex window. This former resident of madame B's in the town of S-D has a reputation for hating children. I also liking cats. Enough not to have one. That overconfident ground-floor Potter with chocolate Lab named Latte feigning shock when I told her that. She's from The Outers, so instead of the friendly tangled back courtyards we used to have, now looking down from Settler-Nun flats onto North America's biggest crop: lawn. Hours get spent artfully arranging plastic lawn sets shaped like dinosaurs in it. Her chocolate Lab following her all day, nuzzling nuzzling trying to get attention. Occasionally she throwing a crumb his way, just enough for keeping addicted.

But whatever inciting me to say my name means French pet, diminutive of multiple layers + possibilities? Rest assured, dear X, a tale's encrypted mid all these future comings + goings of parlour queens, telephone girls, leather divas, Grandpa's little split-tailed fis'. A tale unspeakable as owls in ceaseless vigil staring from eyes round + amber as that cat Etta's [more of whom soon]. Please be further advised, only epiphanic afternoons shall herein be remembered. Circumstantially, I am posturing as woman of inchoate origin [problematically, I can hear you saying]. To underscore how we are haunted by secrets of others. Such as they colporting spite from The Outers to rue Settler-Nun, Mile-End, QC. Further absorbing under surface of community amenity, bitter particles of those going there before--the *Shale Pit Workers*! Floating up from burnt-down Crystal Palace, whose rotting pylons still directly under. Where once upon a time, when it not being used for smallpox hospice, British officers used to hold their

balls.

They were rumoured not to like girls like me very much.
They also hated Indians.
This is better documented.
By the end of our tale, we may likewise be ~~dead~~

Increasingly I am slipping. Yesterday, riding bicycle down sidewalk, past deserted bank building, sticking middle finger straight up in fuck-you sign a former prime minister made famous. I liking best when he wearing fringed jacket + paddling a canoe. Trying by slightly bending th' digital to make th' sign without, in my case, anybody noticing. A thin man, very dark eye shadows looking straight into my face. As if 'Are you crazy?' 'Oh non·non non,' I saying waving both hands in air, in somewhat accented French. 'This not meant for you!' Turning right + driving, still on sidewalk, past where th' bank machine now is, recounting whole incident in rather loud voice to myself. But th' worse glissement of thought toward inappropriate action happening th' other day on bus. Sitting there in dim light called pénombre in a chambre, I seeing outline of breast just like *hers* + nearly reaching out + cupping. Which confusion of proprieties I blaming on incident with ~~Brother Language~~ Untel. Little conflagrations flaring up in dark. Like lightning in a film noir.

Face looks out the window. Passers hurrying by, already bearing regifted Xmas packages, pretending not to notice. Behind it the Room. Railway-flat arched double decorated with plaster-leafed scrolling. Butt-dowelled ceiling angels. In dark stairway outside Room door, a bent silhouette in peaked Paris gendarme pillbox's watching through keyhole. We are for the moment hard put to say what he is doing there. A library shelf holds books in French + English + a few in a script not European. Plus various family groupings significant to our ~~Native~~ narrator. On a work table closer to the window, but not too close because of brats screaming thin as credit Down Below♥, one of those old computers that look like squashed soccer balls. Grey-+-turquoise-insets. On a midnight-blue screen a jumbled set of paras. Rescued from the trash.

♥Reader, a copy of Lenore Carrington's *Down Below* lies on Room bedside cube. Recounting incarceration in a Spanish asylum, where a pavilion called Down Below was said to represent life, healing, delight. You have to be ready for such conformity! Rest assured, on quitting autobiographic space, ~~profane~~ material illuminations will propel our intrigue. Say, in bar round corner, guy entering lugging case of 'untaxed' bouteilles de rouge. Inevitably some client at dark corner table shouting dythyrambically: — That's Montreal for you! Do not guy + contraband bottles, glowing with aura of our-town's mythic insubordination, suggest more promising vectors for commencing ?

Telephone rings + *Face*. Retreating into darkness. Vaguely intuiting shadow behind closed stairway door, watching through keyhole. *Don't be paranoid*. Shadow bending + the Parisian cop, for that incongruously's what it is, extricates a loupe, actually a jeweller's glass, gift from his old wartime bud, Double Jos. Dousse, pronounced Deuce, in Pincher Creek, AB, as *Face* reappearing. In keyhole's line of vision. Which *Face* likely not also sensing presence of second cop surveillant, the Québécois assistant, sitting 'gainst wall, seven steps down from kneeling Parisian, unlit cigarette stuck to bottom lip, typing away on a minuscule computer, simultaneously releasing a truly terrible fart, fart slowly expanding to fill entire inner stairway space, framed by chipped black-painted steps, pale walls, shadowy stairway ceiling, full of suspect crooks + crannies. The peaked pillbox above staring as unflinchingly ahead as a ship's captain steering through a storm. His haughty Parisian lip rising in a grimace. These Québécois don't know how to eat. And what a physiognomy! Taut as a boil, thinks the old cop hatefully, who can't stand another physical presence in any closed space.

Face looks out again. Oh darling X. Is not our future narrative to keep us moving forward? Bus, bicycle, cinema streaming up du Parc, in three, four different measures, for avoiding paranoia. So stay put [*Face*] + keep an eye on things while we go to get th' story. Yes. *We* disperse. Often. Dissociation oblige! When certain members behaving. Inappropriately. *She* all crooked on bed in Room's dark end. *I/th' fly* on th' wall. Pretendin' not to notice, beatin' a retreat. Right through crack in Room door panel to dark inner stairway outside Room door. My six legs spread uncomfortably round old Parisian cop's collar. Peekin' through keyhole in position not affordin', erotically, great deal a' pleasure. Peekin' back to where R Surrogate's akimbo, shiny vulve visible in middle, on dark satin sheet. See

She's movin'!

I dance my little jig. Up + down like a man. Round + round like a woman. Vague smell of oyster. X, notwithstandin'♥ your teensy-weensy fear of dénouement: on th' afternoon we are

---

♥A/~~Basement~~ Bottom Historian must guard against overinterpretation. Suffice it to note the term 'notwithstanding' is a defining aspect of our collective. Being chronically invoked [or some equivalent] to cover hesitation or dubiety rooted in our famous fear of offending. Which obsessive considering of all exceptions before proceeding further accounting for the air of surreal gravitas conferred on us by strangers. Mirrored in our Charter, the term Notwithstanding [summoned to defend French-language + other collective rights] is also invoked to override freedom of expression, assembly, freedom from undue search, etc. Which override power is 'temporary,' yet may be re-enacted *indefinitely*!

murdered, this set will turn malodorous. R Surrogate on bed in Room's dim end, at a loss without our 100 compound eyes, our multi-segmented feet for adherin' to ceilin', admirably equipped to assume th' méta-physical under all th' masks, denials, secrets of that Psycho called Reality. Vrai, I mebbe back as a ghose. But let us begin as promised. Someone knockin' on oeil-de-boeuf door. At bottom of stairway. Contemporaneity oblige: it wasn't protection if it didn't have a hole in it.

*

On th' radio, Celia Raw Raw© is talking about th' wonder fullness of family. And American. Marines are ack-ack-bam-splatting desert towns 'exceptionally.' —*I sure wouldn't've liked to be in that compound we bombed*, quoth th' general. Human embryos are being cloned noli me tangere — I mean nolo contendere — for therapeutic purposes. Nobody can resist. Down Below, on corner of Settler-Nun + Dada-Jesus, beside a plastic outer banister, formerly wrought iron, snaked up with 50s-style Christmas synecdoches, the tow-headed Potter's waiting for the light. Her chocolate Lab sniffing at her cunt. Looking quickly to the left, to the right, like guy waiting to cross street trying to slip hand in pocket + adjust balls without anybody noticing, she mounts the dog's back.

Il neige. Il neige. Il neige. Under a sky ethereally white with somewhat out-of-focus Greek goddess, I/Rosine pedalling up crowded av. du Parc. Dragging my foot on th' sidewalk, citizen that I am, not bumping into anyone. Past th' old Belgian Chocolate man, white art-nouveau columns of Librairie R-B, ex-silent cinema♥ stripped of all its marbles. When bus #80 pulling up. Th' driver already having his pine boughs out. Rosine [her heart!] was in Chicago. His ticket well of jellybeans, he was offering to strangers. Continuing North, knowing he'd be yelling out th' streets, festooning them in their functional reality: —*Laurier, rue des magasins dispendieux. Saint-Viateur, Bagel Street. Tous ceux qui veulent s'acheter des bagels, svp descendre icitte.* Liking liquorice as I do, getting on to stick my fingers in his mix. But th' pine boughs being a distant *trop* in th' memory, backing out between folding doors, adjusting my vis-on in convex mirror, I admonishing him for that.

♥ Let's let speak for themselves those hats worn by women attending, ca. 1921, modish av. du Parc art-nouveau cinema, whose still pristine high white-tiled + columned façade contemporaneously fronting book + bauble establishment, Librairie RB (after Roland Barthes). Where in époque, ladies' hats taut with ghosts of creatures and fauna going there before [beaver, whole birds, dried berries in little leather sacs, fur, etc.], berated by modest scions of 'pied-noir' Shale Pit Workers! + 'nombrils-jaunes' tannery employees in cheaper seats behind. For 'occupyin' space.'

—*Femme la potte ma belle*, he yelling, triple chin turning left/right, tongue sticking out like taxi dispatcher's, sliding over elle's on th' phone si l'on exigeai-t-une-macheen immediate-ly—*Oui-i-i madame ... qu'elle est adorâb*! Tongue between lips in fake sensual anticipation. Same fleshy lips as Paris cop's stagiaire, contorted into tight stairway corner, a Montréal Pool Room 'steamie' fermenting in his gut, who, eyes closed in pain, letting go another, then, notwithstanding derrière's cruel enjambment on cutting edge of paint-chipped inner middle step: falling asleep. Having puffed a joint for dessert, all by himself, outside l'École nationale de théâtre, the assistant's nodding, halfway down inner 4999 Settler-Nun stairway, whose façade, red-orange painted brick, pressed peeling metal cornice, reading 1908 in middle, curiously resembling a dollhouse: one little brick floor piled atop another. Up up up. Yet, numbered downward, to bottom, #4995 directly over buried pylons of former magnificent Crystal Palace, built for agricultural + commercial exposition purposes. Where ca. 1885, mid rows of faces on iron beds erupting like plastic bubbles into fetid putrid pus, lying Shale Pit Workers! of neighbouring Saint-John-Baptiste, dying in smallpox epidemy, raging in our filth-+-vice-ridden city. The 'night soil' not yet bein' plucked from alleys, overflowin' + floatin', thawin', joined by offal, floatin' downhill from overflowin' privies, down lanes where children playin' in first warm April suns. Further contaminatin' leakage from refuse barrels, vegetable leavin's, broken sewers, all rushin' in filthy ruisseaux. As if to welcome pestilence just steppin' off th' train. Which Palace's wooden walls, quarantined for duration, catchin' spark from carriage house one hot June night +

burnin'
down.

Real light of day. Likewise falling through oeil-de-boeuf onto upper palier of stairway. Where old cop, Casse-Noisette to his friends, on knees, awaiting, en principe, as befitting diplômé de l'École Supérieure de Police de Paris: a search warrant. Mind-surfing with instinct of the melancholic, for whom phantoms = prime companions, o'er neighbourhood, o'er succeeding generations of recurring genetically torqued brats born on former Crystal Palace site, o'er former orchards + fields + men + this + that. Till *Face*, in streaking past Room door keyhole, causing Parisian's shoulders, gaunt as a skeleton's, to settle rapidly, provocatively, into Eureka position. Sensing, with déjà vu of the passionately committed, some faint hint or code reminiscent of the remarquable nez of old wartime bud DJ Dousse, ce danseur à claquettes, sent to France to entertain les troupes, who declaring one steamy day, in Café Brecht, rue Belloc, 8ᵐᵉ, in Paris, little fluffs of fog floating by window, that th'good people of Pincher Creek, AB'd dubbed his, Double Jos.'s proboscis:

Iroquois Falls.

The gendarme's face melts like wrinkles in a darkened mirror. A beatitudinous smile. Remembering Jos.'s tanned slender —

We are loath to go ~~Father~~ farther. Being

Increasingly afraid. Of yielding to our time. But maybe time is ripe? Parking R bike under th' spilling maple, taking outer stairs two at a time, holding high torrefacteur espresso-grind Réveille-Toi coffee, heureusement not meeting Neighbour [aka th'landlord], yesterday hissing on landing: —*I could get you out of here if I wanted.* Exhibiting tongue, curved at th' root + further accusing, in disgusted tone-of-knowing, I/R, daughter of Veeera, of stealing her *Book of Genocides*. Feeling brave, slamming oeil-de-boeuf door, ascending eerie inner stairs, dark as a crypt, I/R entering railway-flat Room, musky plaster walls oozing dusky comfort of person-not-homeless, + removing dusty yellow jacket of th' *Book of Genocides* from shelf. Lent possibly inchoately [people were freer then] after you my darling X, being from ailleurs, forgetting triplexes♥ in Saint-Louis-du-Mile-End having TWO sets of stairs. Outside. Plus inner, dropping directly down from upper flat door. Shoving I/R out gently. I clopped. I clopped. I clopped. Reaching for *Book of Genocides*, turning non-acid-treated leafs. Detaching as I touching. GER-many. Somalia. Armenia. Rwanda. Kosovo. Sudan. Eeeeeeeast Teeeeeeemor. Scrutinizing for la Gêne on which we standing, those going here before, stencilled in ice tunnel below bridge. Leading to where children fished + cows drank from grassy slopes ere THAT DAMN RESERVE CEMENTED IN FOR SEAWAY. But. Never say you're an Indian. If. You're. Not. Did not Auntie Dill, sitting on her scooter outside Starby's in Kelowna, her useless foot in stiletto slingback sticking out horizontally in front, reply when asked what colour Grandma's hair was, hint of panic beneath her perfect curled lashes:

    —N-O-T N-O-I-R.

♥If material conditions shape the spirit, we may empirically declare the Triplex the place where what is happening is the place. To wit: climbing those over-romanticized outside stairs, rising curved or straight from court up up brick or stone façade, it's as if walking toward the sky. Moreover, after climbing first flight to façade middle, one's confronted, stepping through second gallery door, by yet another private inner stairway to topmost entrance: We are proud of this architectural peculiarity, where each exit, no matter how high, permitting unique access to exterior. So every wife may call her flat her house.

Things were NOT. Going well. I/R, friend, lover, former fur-coat model in Austin, Texas, reporter, writer of futuristic pamphlets, having aroused ressentiment round court, full of plastic dinosaurs, for washing, with leather friend D, our plastic toys [a very vanilla selection, th' blue electric, veined, realistic, staff choice at Good Vibrations, th' leather harness + recyclable condom with bumps] on balcony. Th' breeder screaming up from alley it not nice for th' children. Which ressentiment increasing per annum. And. Being unable to oppose time + maybe time is ripe. Turning pages of landlord's *Book of Genocides*. And finding no mention of that Gêne on which we ourselves standing — les cent-cinquante-millions — vrai, I/R never thinking of that before. Silent. Like falling snow on mountains. Letting th' yellowed leaves fly one by one. Out window. Then felt a wave of shame. And went to lie down.

Got up again. A ~~turd~~ hurly-gurly. Peeking behind venetians. At th' yellowed pages mingling with autumn leaves as large as yellow hands. Floating down block of recent Yuppie proprietors, down block of more anarcho weedier front yards, prevailing late millennium. O'er former Palace grounds, whence th' Shale Pit Workers!, after work, coming to wash feet. In fountain. Drinking caribou + singing. *Oh th' shale pit workers/like to take a swig*. O'er th' avenue. Th' stretch of common. With robin. O'er man taking picture of th' emptiness in th' centre of th' city. Landing at foot of that old Con-fed Father, George Cartier's monument.

X, though this novel seemingly set in an apartment, awkward as 3-D set of *Dial M for Murder*, it actually taking place on a bus. We break up. Very painful, but maybe don't. You, my tender, having written by February your journey over. And here it is next November. Getting up from back horizontal bus seat, shaking dress, grey wool melton, covering to ankles, copped from a nun, but that's another story. I rang + rang + RANG. Till driver slamming brakes + I/R landing, malheureusement akimbo, in field near gazebo. Sure enough, round old Cartier's feet, winged atop his obelisk, yellowed pages of th' *Book of Genocides* flew. I/R pursuing o'er th' avenue, ample grey shirring round ankles, into parc Settler-Nun [formerly F's Field]. After orchard growing there. Blossoms in spring. Floating down like snow flying in gentle breeze off Royal-Mount beside. Down. Down. Gathering th' yellowed leaves one by one. Though containing no mention of people camping there ere establishment of Gentleman's Raquette + Hunt, then glass-+-iron Crystal Palace's mille-et-une facettes, central nef — notwithstanding Palace's exposition vocation — reserved for skating. And daring circus acts. Saltimbanques! ~~FOUFOUNES~~ FUNAMBULES♥ saying French. In summers, outside its softwood lumber walls [addended locally, in departure from perfect crystalline effect of British Mother Country model, for climate], British officers strolling mid fountains where the Shale Pit Workers!, pieds noirs, washing feet + drinking caribou, in paper bags, while singing:

O th' shale-pit workers
Big or small
Are not proud people
They like to take a swig
They spare nothing to have fun in summer
It'll be rough
Getting through th' winter

But never on a Sunday, when, hair combed back with water, fertile lips, chins, soaped skin under frayed

---

♥The stroller making said onomatopoeic error would be a language-challenged Anglo. Walking 'Sainte-Cat' East, past the black defenestered Goth-scrawled home to Québécois punk. Unable to hear difference between French 'ou' [said oo] + French 'u' [y]. Thus, confusing *Foufounes Électriques* [Electric Asses] with Funambules Électriques [Electric Circus]. Which Anglo, in strolling, possibly recalling dead punk diva Kathy Acker performing there [in English]. Shaved, pierced, tattooed, boot toes turned in for focus, muttering sotto voce: —*I hate readings*. Outside church opposite, similar-coded homeless kids milling famished round Father Pop's van. For coffee.

ironed shirts, boys on way to mass, bifurcating in wake of some skinny waist of a girl into orchard at parc's south end. Having, so story going, kissed her in stairway, rue Coloniale:

He leans her back on trunk. Headiness of blossoms. Bees buzzing round. Boy rubbing slowly gently against. Hairless cheek caressing downiness of neck. Shirt + dress undone, torso a torso. Panties slightly lowered. Th' orchard exhales its sweetness. Taking out his nob, he fritti-frotting fragrant bloomer crotch. Her shaking fingers helping pull them off. In those days no question of unproductive sperm. He didn't care. Did she. Slips it in her wetness. Past some little obstacle, oh th' softness of her folds. Nothing to. Compare. Slip slide slip slide in soft stay out. Her feet were off th' ground. He impaled her, hard, determined. Not too rapid! Her mouth open, he kissed it. They were catching every drop of pleasure.

—*A love child*! screaming Auntie Dill. Rocking in her chair.

They also held the Caledonian Games there ...

There, there —

Day's Last Real Light

Falls o'er th' casement. Casting hard truths on ~~feces~~ *Face*
barely visible in upper Settler-Nun window. *—Hey! Stay
put [Face] while we go to get th' story!* Yes, we disburse.
Often. For reason of. Serotonin. Bumping on bed. Like
you X, you little diapered baby, pretending to be Bottom.
Or I/R, still late October, daily exiting 4999 Settler-Nun
+ climbing up to bar at 4848 boul Saint. Cloche hat.
Relaxed flowing skirt. Similarly turned-out millennials
climbing even higher. Past arched bar door to Lili St-Cyr
revival. Which inimitable showgirl disrobing, ca. 1940,
on Sala Rossa stage. Wiith long golden mane. Holding
pheasant, fanning out obligingly. Under glimmering red
star of worker solidarity.♥

♥Ah, that high red star over Sala Rossa stage. Not to be taken for mere rem-
nant of pre-war socialist hubris. When Jewish Worker Circle's new 4848 boul
Saint building's modernist façade doors first opening on people climbing to
topfloor theatre for very inspiring events [Eleanor Roosevelt spoke there]. Or
the later Centro Social Espagnol's members politicking, dancing. Sometimes
the tango. Their well-fleshed elders to this day sitting down to tapas in stucco
bar on second. While on third the red star with sickle in middle still shining over [grant it] mostly cultural rebels: Electronic Robots. Naughty Beaver
Bingos. Baby Lezzie Strips. [Ladies, if over 40, stay away from the latter: the
younger chicks get nervous, thinking you're a mother.]

But just as our future novel space opening. Wide as the legs of a porn queen. Or straight girl with butch going down on her — oh they do spread for good head — Peter of New York's listing dangerously through Spanish-arched bar door, black coat jerky sideways tangoing toward stucco-skirted counter, empathy patch quivering:

—*Elvira you Uke I love you!*

—*Jewish Uke, dude, there's a difference,* retorting blonde barmaid, space, conspicuous, between teeth.

—*This place's fulla ghosts,* hazarding P [guilty, a little Uke himself]. Reaching, on bias, the crescent stucco bar, anxiously spreading arms + ordering amaretto for all, while sifting versinthed/muscle-relaxed cerebrum for bloody cheap-tweed phantom lying akimbo on long white-tiled basement bathroom floor, acrid-sweet smoke sliding from cubicle row of swinging doors.

—That washroom's right out of *Dial M for Murder*, huh?

Smiling + watching, sideways, the curved bar of amaretto-tipping mouths. For approval. A serendipitous error. To use to our benefit. Peter has served his purpose:

Dial M for Murder

Dear Reader, here we may begin our intrigue. Mid hangers-on, a natural element, gathered under 4999 Settler-Nun darkening third-floor railway-flat window. In the rain. Umbrellas raised smooth, or dehisce, like gangsters at a funeral. Heads shaved or impercipiently coiffed. Turned toward contour behind venetians. Their wildest élans♥ [like Peter's] dutifully restrained. Eagerly awaiting, futurity oblige, a dénouement of some devastating calumny or love tourniquet. —*Entoutkàs*, venturing the café-philosopher among us, goateed + pointedly down at the heel: —*Even if only about love. Are not love's overwrought requiems usually covering deeper pilferings or betrayals, lost lands, homes, or lost people in them?* Meaning our novel beginning drenched in the acerbic, therefore subject to countless deviations + only slowly, anteriorly, releasing its elixir. While on sidewalk, said hangers, 'to a man' faded

♥ Which *élan* [ardour] for scandal + gossip in the second official language [English] if we adhering to the local truism: Catholics like to do; Protestants to watch. Seconded by Jewish Mordecai's *Who knows what thoughts lurk behind those [anglo] porridge faces?* But where in this picture are other Others? Say, those Scots fur traders + their Indigenous wives from long-gone St-Gabriel Métis Presbyterian Church. Were their offspring considered Anglo? Indian? Or enjoying a warm fluidity of situation? Unlikely the latter, for as the reprehensible Burroughs remarking: "What is Panic? The realization that everything's alive [moving!]."

in raiment [+ aspect]. Gazing + unhurriedly opening, closing their odd-shaped umbrellas. Jostled, occasionally, by younger, more productive A-types rushing home to dinner. Who, themselves — if glancing up a sec at *Face* in Settler-Nun window — thinking [being somehow negatively predisposed]: rumour having, a pervert [children look away embarrassed]. While *Face* in situ behind sooty grey venetians denying, like everyone in this theatre, what *is*. And expounding what is not. Vaguely eyeing potlid of clouds. Her little blonde inner princess, raised to th' manner by Grandpa. Standing at oval oak table, liquid eye whites of someone nursed a very long time. Working fingers in flamenco-style movement, trying to ignore guilty wet panties strewn about ankles. — *Th' bee's knees*, screaming Auntie Dill protectively. Veeera looking disgusted. Taking brush + roughly pulling tangles from Rosie's astonishing albino curls. While Maddie [th' auntie in th' know] lighting cigarette + declaring I/little R potentially th' double of that star in Hitchcock's *Dial M for Murder*, th' future Princess Grace of Monaco: Blonde. Curly. Dripping in brightness + shadow. Which star, guilelessly admitting she killing, knowing innately — *like every bourgeois opportunist*, adding Maddie [a Trotskyist] — th' value of seeming candid. But:

Let them discourse, th' passers
If it relieving their spirits!
X, speaking of dénouement:
Why I/R forgetting
The soft lips of French boys
At townhall 'soirées dansantes' in Valleyfield
By bowing to your fragrant second landscape
On cliff at Grandpapa's ranch
Overlooking th' Columbia.

Such *bowing*! Mocking ex-friend Agathe of Sainte-Agathe, herself named after th' mountain town named after th' Sainte, kicking th' valise with silver box of Grandmaman's ashes she daily taking out + stroking, under th' bed. Such *bending*, laughing Agathe, uncorking cold blanc + passing th' sardines, that last hot afternoon, wide-set eyes moving side to side. As if knowing, full well, cette anglaise ~~after her man~~ no real lezzie. Not to mention, on occasion, even pretending to be Native. To pass with th' Francos. Agathe, crossing her perfect pedicured feet. And pouring, with well-groomed hand of classic séductrice, th' cold white into gleaming goblet, th' fan blowing air, cheeks, hair, in white stucco, not to mention impeccable, kitchen, one tiny dollhouse room opening on another, through to th' court, beyond which one more vista of flats, likewise ironstaircased in back, reaching North for blocks. —Such bending *aside, you, Rosine, like the rest of us, pining after that thing that, in nuzzling, moving women's thighs so directly!*

But let us stick to the path of our intrigue. Rue Settler-Nun, Mile-End, QC. Named after the first convent founder [herself never taking the veil]. Greasy with autumn leaves + freezing rain. Under the slithering feet of the socially ascendant, migrating from The Outers + buying workers' flats. *Starter houses* they calling them [are not their horizons unlimited?]. Whose rebuilt balconies + terrasses extending under adjacent rent-controlled windows. For bar-b-cues in summer. While in winter, their parade of suede or leather coats. Hats. Authentic fur-lined flaps. Pressed cashmere scarves. Kid-gloved fingers grasping gym bags or grocery organics, traipsing North. Abruptly turning into courts + opening doors on whatever ambience surviving the renos.

Oppositely, our hangers, having stared up a time at *Face* or facsimile behind railway-flat pane. Continuing shuffling South, boul Saint. Direction, La Cabane Copa Biftek Bobards Blizzarts Double Deuce Vice Piscine Main-Drain Coco-Coquette. Raising frayed or ironed collars. Lighting, on nearing wood-door thresholds, cigarettes.

With gestures of travellers stuck in pleasant dislocating space of dreams. Spurred by liminal refreshments [use your veeza for purchase]. Which purchase, accomplished, is disquietude avoided. Peaks. Solicitations. —*Èvelyne, the night is young! Our town salutes you!* Blurring in drift to prochain appeasement. All systems screaming —*It must not be hoarded!* Some digressing through iron turnstiles. Into bathhouse, rue Napoléon. Cedar boughs for flogging. Or toward establishment farther North, corner Dada-Jesus. Where berserk rapist, earlier fleeing cops, melting into steam-room fogging upper storey blue bay windows. Causing [tourist later tweeting] *yours truly to be thrown down inside bathhouse stairs. Ere Golden Glove boxer giving two nice shiners. Every franco fuck's extorting us Americans.* Landing on sidewalk. Where more hairy-scary but mostly inconsequential dudes. Comedically performing ostentatious scams, using local onomatopoeia [Gallic, yet fricative to point of unfathomable]. Backlit in car-flickering façades dissolving to dark-shrouded fantasmagoric cornices, pediments, orbs, beavers. Inset stars of David. The headlights, in parking, sliding o'er street-level dusty plastic, wigged, besequined [or faded] displays in shop windows. Sparkling with malice.

However, ca. 4p, on this day of our lord, November 6, 2003, one hanger degageant from those trudging South toward the action. Turning sparse goatee North toward still lit pink + grey horizon. Is not his girlfriend pregnant? Meaning newly embracing theories regarding necessary cohesiveness of family unit. Wanting at almost 50 to be a parent, whatever accumulated ~~dependencies~~ risks + means of paying. Shuffling away from cohorts after raising shaved [tattooed] head, buttoning frayed wool under chin + muttering [perhaps smugly]: —This bi'd de'd? Having noticed *Face* behind the louvres at precise same angle as earlier this morning. Eyes fixed like cameo's, West toward the mountain. —*Oh mark how the shifting winds from west arise. And what collected night involves the skies!* he citing. Resuming Northbound shuffle, toward little flat + grow-op. Overlooking factories. Dimly in perspective. On edge of horizon.

—*Or is that frost on the pane?* wondering younger expensively sport-togged passer. Hopeful, sardonic [profession, reporter]. Skittling o'er gravelly icy surface, o'er stuck half-frozen pages of *Book of Genocides* [Armenia, Rwanda]. Pushing fat-matching-red-chanvre snowsuit in stroller. Recalling seeing that *Face* in upper window at Saint-Jean-Baptiste street fête last summer. Mixing drinks in little booth, simultaneously, repetitively, turning slightly receding chin. Toward 4999 Settler-Nun landlord, arriving from dacha, stepping down from jeep. In magnificent hand-woven poncho. Immediately sidling over + whispering 'confidentially' in ear of that tow-headed Potter from Oregon. Living on bottom. Whose Lab, Chocolate Latte, always nuzzling nuzzling at her.

The reporter continuing forcing stroller North. Over hillocks of salt-loosened slush. Stepping faster past anarchist's place on corner. Who sneering at her on Saint-Jean fête day last summer: —*A journalist? Ha! Always betraying the literary. With your shitloads of common sense.* That day, so hot, it almost melting macadam. Still, people doing Argentinean tango. Foxtrot. Singing folk songs under sky suddenly darkening. Then

John Cage thunderclap, the woman

Remembering thinking. Shivering a little. Having done her day of freelance work. Researching human population explosion impact on wheat streak mutations. Contributing to ever-increasing gluten intolerance. Having also jogged once around the parc. Having partaken of end-of-aft latte at Café Nous. Ere gathering little Axel from best faubourg daycare. Generously subsidized, for, in Québec [nearly a republic], children are everything. Shivering, as if afraid. Though everything [in life] ostensibly okay. Icy rain even relenting a little. As two clouds, in spreading, emitting low

31

pink ray. Projecting full charge of light on Settler-Nun brick. An effect of cut-into-ribbons, thinking the reporter [like everyone of her station, wannabe novelist]: blue. Yellow. Purple.

Suddenly brushing Settler-Nun venetians. Striating Room, long + narrow, like all flats in the 'hood, with dark prison-bar effect. Same closed-in effect as in *Dial M for Murder*. With its claustrophobic vertically pleated velvet curtains. The fussy hand of the husband obsessively opening + closing. Cause plotting to kill, for purpose of retrieving mojo from that expensive bitch he marrying. —*My wife has the money*, he whining to hired assassin, an inept second-hand car salesman. Nodding with own s-somewhat inad-ad-equate ch-chin toward l-lush velvet-draped interior: the s-s-settees, the l-lamps. A scene less cinema than theatre. The future crime being rehearsed repetitively. Ere happening in inverse.

Darkness a moment.

Ray, single, filtered, striking casement once more. Jazzy, ephemeral, like all things of beauty. Pausing a click, as if cinematically insisting on darkness in 4999 Settler-Nun middle. Pullulating with timeless ressentiments + secrets. Seeping from fissures in ancient painted-over wallpaper. From cracks in oversanded, badly slanting floors. Laid ca. 1900. By mostly Catholic builders. On burnt-down

Crystal Palace grounds. But soon leased, or mortgaged. Chiefly by Protestants. Some, scions of les nombrils jaunes, former tannery workers. Whom franco Shale Pit Workers! beating up so vigorously. City edict expressly forbidding bagarres between Anglo [or immigrant] tannery boys + Francos from farther East. Living in tiny unplumbed walk-ins opening directly onto street. Obscure back courts a-reek with the facilities. And at night, notwithstanding those nailed planks blocking bedroom doors, cries of rats. Trying to get in.

    Face looks out again.

But was that Agathe I scoping earlier? Passing in sheered shorty jacket. Leopard stockings, matching leopard cap. Maybe missing I/R's formerly intriguing if paradoxical ways. R ~~faux~~-confidential laugh + slippy-slidey sentences, switching♥ this way + that. Parading smiley down sidewalk,

---

♥ Reader, a lapsus carries a secret index. Little by little revealing why we meandering in speaking. As disparate in associations as a voyageur on a train. Hallucinating on various angles of the sunset, unless distracted by fussy table linen, or fancy brickwork on stations of the early era. When this still new, therefore allegorical, mode of transport advancing in winter night over 'empty' prairie. Direction, a Southern AB smalltown station, where 'copasetic' [i.e., assimilated] young 'half-breed' signalman in stepping out to switchpost, slipping on ice right down under oncoming train. — *Some idiot*, yelling Dill, *'d put salt around th' post.*

secretly deriding all th' little families. Vel-cro, we calling them, clutching their hyper-vitamined babies, swaddled in th' plastic they using in disposables, calling anxiously from balconies. —*Bye-bye kiss-kiss miss-miss. Watch your step. Don't fall.* To whatever departing aunties cousins siblings. Not to mention th' husbands, on Saturdays wrapping in winter styrofoam little pointy-pruned Versailles-style cedars they importing from The Outers. Plus fixing bars to windows. To protect from ecological minimals. Staggering, early on a Sunday, up from th' parc. Girl, very stoned. Clinging to guy + screaming in French, high to point of éclatement:

—*I always wonder why couples holding on like that!*

Agathe slippy-sliding along with little pot-bellied man. Maybe, on looking up a second, regretting that day last September, pouring little glass of blanc + telling I/R so sweetly: —*It's what you've come to in life.* Agathe + her man advancing gingerly up street. Each [covertly] glancing back a second. Agathe choosing words to dissuade her Boubou completely, in case he still pining after that so-called lezzie in upper casement window: —*People if cut off from their roots. Growing unreliable. Unstable.* The pair, for some months together again. Continuing North, content. Under clouds seeming ever darker. More ominous. Cause

On every kitchen radio, news of coming ice storm.

Meaning first wave of suppertime eagers descending earlier than usual. From bus #97, Mont-Royàl East. Starting up street, tightening scarves + plunging gloved hands in pockets. One, a lady borough councillor, mouse in her purse she taming to prevent from chewing kitchen. Herself, in glancing up at 4999 Settler-Nun window, musing that *Face* behind venetians permanently staring toward yonder mountain. Which mountain named, like the avenue, Mont-Royàl in French. Yet, interestingly, 'Monte Reale' [Italian] providing the name for our French-speaking [sort of] agglomerate. The skies, as she advancing, abruptly spewing freezing rain. Soon to be ice-coating all externals, inc. thin cotton shoulders of howling coatless girl barrelling up Settler-Nun macadam. Crying: —*You're going to be sorry/For leaving me in this area!*

Her thin-clad person stamped by electric light slicing ever sharper through window lace or venetians. Settling in bas relief on broken pavement. Garbage. Two blowing pages. From *Book of Genocides* [Eritrea, Somalia]. Frozen gutter water. Flowing from alley. Over which man leaping unsteadily. Ere turning right into court + slowly up rickety iron steps. Daily quart of Slernoff's bien entamé in pocket. On good days downing even more. All there is available. Notwithstanding recent bad experience, having grown dozy in his bath. Stepping out + slipping to floor —

naked whale of a form becoming stuck between parabolic slope of tub. And oppositely curving enamel contour of toilet. So wife, after tugging + pulling. Ashamedly calling upstairs neighbour — burly lineman with handsome black moustache. Who commenting from Slavoj's narrow bathroom door. — *Gosh, 'Lana, I'll need th' winch.*

While from the alley, the gutter stream, icing on surface, but still meandering under. O'er rue Settler-Nun, direction, av. du Parc. Where, in upper rear window, shrink named MacBeth [more on whom imminently], contrary to those who on entering their premises, lighting up to maximum, extinguishing his halogen. The better to scope slender boy-ass in crack-junkie camouflage. Stepping from alley into traffic. For purpose of squeegeeing windshields. Stepping back again. A rhythm going on for hours. The kid's feet, in retreating to sidewalk, slipping. Entangling feet of yet another passer:

The Poet. Who, in glancing from corner of her retina, intuiting — being poet — that as with stars, as with, alas, love itself, the potency of an object dimming proportionately the more one casting full gaze upon it. And knowing skeletal youth with squeegee. In reality of his context: the traffic, too polluted, exhausted. To be scary. Still, quickening her pace. Up first block, then second. Toward cat Etta's owl gaze. In vigil, in Poet's own upper railway-flat window. Though Etta's olfactories now in hyperextensive alert. Due to rancid decaying odour from next-door 4999 Settler-Nun stairwell. Where the old Parisian surveillant hovering ghostlike at upper flat keyhole. While, seven steps down, a fresher junior-cop fetor driving cat's ears back almost horizontal. Her little form further disagreeably absorbing shifting densities, dots, vibrations, on junior sleuth's tiny purple monitor:

> In the kitchen you can smell Uncle Peee[t]. The blood on his raincoat. He smiles through the gap in his teee[t]. Head listing sideways. Miming, for Mama[n], man unresisting shooting tiny 'heasant he now fake fawningly holding up to her. Oh tay says Grandma. She is camping as Victorian . . . .

Then Etta's cat ears relaxing. For, certain familiar very alluring scent. Nearing court gate. Not pheasant, the promise of fish. Faintly wafting from person of her beloved mistress. Along with acrid odours of other hurrying blue- + white-collar workers: hospital receptionist [halitosis]. Shoe-store salesman [flat aftershave + body odour]. Esthetician [tea tree + lavender]. All climbing stairs + opening wooden logement doors. Their windows, renovated French-style cedar or cheap-aluminun-cause-still-rent-controlled flats. Casting evening shadows via half-shut curtains or venetians. On shiny, ever icier street.

Two Blocks Over, MacBeth

[Therapist] awaits. Splotchy Celtic-French face with touch of Huron in it [not unusual in this place]. Splendidly framed in steel-curved-at-the-corners window. Only remaining late-deco casement in this revivalist dump. By April, his cozy little office ~~will have~~ to be [he hates the future anterior] requisitioned. For language college under. Entoutkàs, the place already ruined. [Here, MacBeth makes a moue.] Save, dieu merci, inner stair rail's sleek gold horizontal arrows. Winding round oval plaster corners painted — quelle horreur — baby blue. But

Who's that knocking at the gate?

Through faint-grey pane in bright still mid-afternoon light: low in-grate buildings. Restaurant supplies. Tuxedos. Weddings. Leopard Costume Rentals. Traffic, av. du Parc: souped, battered, glittery or ratty, 20 percent junkie, you can tell by the shuffle. *Whom we, for peace, have treated poorly.* His favourite, Rosie, late. —*Your option*, he telling her. Yet wishing to

Cure her of that!
Canst thou not minister to a mind diseas'd

Pluck from the memory a rooted sorrow
Raze out the written troubles of the brain?

At least she's fairly named: Rose. Notwithstanding the practice, in different regions, of naming little twats variants thereof: Rosella in Bouctouche, Ro-zanne in Sainte-Bonne, Rose Rose in Hoche-Maison, Rosine [she ultimately asserting] after old postcard in Veeera's drawer of Wiertz's *La Belle Rosine*. Talking pleasantly with her skeleton. The therapist, globe in his hand to keep from washing them again, twirling on heel + sitting gingerly at parabolic amber École du meuble de Montréal desk. And, being man both frivolous + metaphysical, copying in minuscule script in minuscule moleskin of the type used by Hemingway + co. A page on platinum laptop monitor she sending from diary:

I/Rosine hiking in Puerto Barriada. Incredible green cliffs plunging to sea. Narrow path along precipice. I am sufferingfrom vertigo. Afraid X [you bitch], prancing like mountain goat behind, will push me off.

Straightening [nothing aging like poor posture], the shrink's raising a scratchy cheek. Trousered in sybaritic British tweed, baggy at knees. Against the smoky window:

39

crackling of leaves. He's loving how Météo Québec showing coming pluie glaçante as tiny acute triangles. Writing [wanting to wash hands]:

Absence per se not the essence of a tragedy. True, with every libidinal throe preceding the exquisite moment of passing, pleasure's performed as pain. The question being, in the case of the dissociate, or of any child having parents whose talk not complementing the interior who-am-we: What part of her at any [usually erotic] instigation crossing the great divide? What part [if any] left to speak?

Raising another cheek + listening: no footsteps — only distant yé-yé radio in baby-blue hall. He writes:

She's a fake. Like everyone in this place.

The Room

I sit at my desk. ~~Middle aged + Unrepentant~~. On bookshelf above: the family portrait. Three dark sisters sitting on sofa, heads up, chins pert, pointing to-morrow. Husbands, pale-eyed Scot., Germ., Brit., respectively: trying to pay attention. Ten exquisitely turned-out children. I/little R in salmon dress with striped insets flaring down from hips. Liquid round or almond eyes staring into camera. Only one child smiling. Uncle Peeet, slick, moustached. In frame to right of family grouping. Listing lee in white naval officer uniform tap-dancing with guy he calling 'Th' Indian.' To right of Peeet, th' cousins. Hair teased like country-western stars. High cheekbones. Generously made-up.

— *Why've you got those prostitutes up there? Eh? Eh?* [th' Neighbour (aka th' landlord)]

— *Elles se ressemblent a mes cousines!* [Agathe of Sainte-Agathe]

Was not everyone in th' family, when putting on wire-rimmed glasses + smiling, looking like a cross between 'French-intellectual' + 'Edmonton-cowboy'? --*Know what you want + go where people will notice*, saying th' queen selling punk German shoes in shoe shop behind th' false front, like th' set of a western movie. In strip mall in

41

Haeckville, AB. [Where you, X, with your 100-watt amber eyes, sending I/R for ice. While sneaking into photo shop for prints of rival spread generously on grass.] We were always on th' move. Forever crossing border at sunset. From Judith, or Butte, MT. In Buick, Jeep, Caddy. Signs saying BRIGHTEN UP. WELL-AGED MANURE. STONY PLAIN SEED-CLEANING PLANT. Capable of taking some thin pyramid-type steel structure trussed up there in distance. By Shell, Petro Can, Esso. For th' Eiffel Tower. Grandpa, th' danseur a claquettes. And also later Peeet. Claiming to have danced at th' Moulin Rouge. Between this fait-glissade + reality were intermediary stages. Not necessarily traceable. Belting down highways. Lucky Chinook arches, hovering over Winnebagos. Planes. —CHARRETTES♥, yelling little Rosie from rear leather seat of Uncle Peeet's jeep.

—*Musta been very far back*, snorting Dill.

♥ Children take words from the air, ventriloquizing omissions passed down generations. Hence Rosie's 'charrettes' possibly those Métis Red River carts, famous for squeaky wooden axles + clanging pots + pans as routed Métis fleeing over rutted prairie. Is not landscape the supreme historian? Ever repeating? Thus: Métis farmer decrying on radio floodbanks raised to keep provincial capital Winnipeg burghers safe. Meaning waters formerly rising on floodplain some genius planned the capital city on flooding outlying hard won back Métis farmer's land instead.

Sliding into booth in joint Northa Vulcan. Brown prairie grass. Ducks swimming clouds in sky-blue ponds. Run by pair of grim-faced Bavarians. Showcases of rosy-cheeked knick-knacks. Had not th' family once upon a time set out from Lachine? By canoe. Knit socks. Blessed crosses. Fleeing smallpox epidemy [ca. 1885]. Stopping + going. All over continent. Once, Grandpa saying, they even allotted deed to main street in Denver. Didn't know it'd be th' main street then.

Somehow they lost it.

—*We coulda been millionaires!*

Not unlike thoughts of youth skirting, ca. 1918, limestone piles + rudimentary sewers. Onto foot-thronging av. *Royàl-Moun'*, he calling it. Sidestepping créature pushing buggy of screechers. Good tan. Sideburns. Pressed shirt starched presque neuve. Under open skin coat. Gold chain. Swinging nonchalantly. Young J. Dousse, born + bred in the West, but wanting to make of fortune his time, pausing opposite #204 Royàl-Moun's tarred four-by-fours under deep-sloped roof. Two small garrets. Spiral outside stairs to tiny second-floor apartment. Built by quarry men, on coming down from Témiscamingue, Blanc-Sablon, Chicoutimi, low with traditional ski-slope roof curving out + up at eaves in wide generous sweep over street to keep snow from crashing down on passers. Houses sometimes abandoned in fleeing smallpox epidemy = youth straightening as Grandpa warning in ear that time, like in dreams, always destroying. Till in future, only one saggy little wing-roofed edifice, corner Mentana, left. Its heart-framed girls dancing embossed on brick in shadow of cottage's extraordinarily excrescent winged gutter. Was not his grandpa's old #204 slated to make way for first Montréal Forum. Built ca. 1920 but soon abandoned by storied hockey *Canadiens* for smoother ice downtown. So arena reverberating, instead, with cheering Commie-leaning Norman Bethune rallies. Then site, those post-war years of hot vacated summer streets, cum pool-hall, lunch-bar, shoestore, rat-painted-corner exterminator. Mutating encore one dark premillennial night. To burnt-out ruin. Making way for current point of rally: giant food emporium. Outside which, on very day of our lord, November 6, 2003: the camouflage kid nearly quaffed. Stepping from curb to squeegee zigzaggy BMW fleeing prone Irish sport. Just run over corner de Maisonneuve. *Anywayee* [people saying], kid only still alive. Cause

Sleeping chez maman.

But on that retrospective 1918 Mile-End spring day, time's only sign in uncharacteristically balmy air: Royàl-

Moun's prematurely budding apples. Winding redolent from orchard up the avenue. Past leaf-obscured speakeasies. Toward Our Lady of Snowy Angels Cemetery. The youth, pausing opposite #204's iron stair, a-clamour with journalists: Anglos loudly proclaiming girl in there suspect. While Francos behind [but not for long], better snipped, bergamotted, to a man, declaring cashier Corinne d'Amour's story of foreigner absconding with $100 from Will-man's cash: vrai. Puis — maudite malchance — very next week, la pauvre petite, in trotting to bank with company's receipts [you can almost see her dainty heels poking dots in snow] shoved by two rogues into conveyance. And waking, sans saccoche, lying on ground. Precisely up there among Our Lady's snowy angels. Maman d'Amour, having opened door of second-level flat, now feebly trying to prevent ces messieurs, as is their nature, from getting foot into reposing daughter's boudoir. As described in *La Patrie* afternoon edition:

> It is in a large white bed in a large bright room that Corinne d'Amour receives us. Wavy brown hair frames her rather large forehead. Her grey eyes still somewhat twinkling; her nose, straight, a little pointed, pink cheeks, but completely pale lips. She whispers they tried to strangle her, pointing at throat, whose white skin

she amicably reveals to show difficulty in swallowing.
We believe she is innocent.

Youth on other side of street. Sporting under beige
twill: giant hard-on.

*

X, you platonic humiliator, on subject of time going its
way [th' delicious crease of your cunt under th' perfumed
folds of your skirt]. Do you remember that day, speeding
down highway somewhere in AB? Chinook arch above.
Your left hand on wheel, your right in my pants. High-
seated trucker braking abreast to watch. True, in future
[anterior], where all stories told, rare is she, who, in
retracing steps of some salty embrace, not feeling stunned
by distance between longing + fulfillment. Causing I/R
to be daily trekking South, direction boul Saint. For
whiling away empty snare of late afternoon. Passing usual
almost empty corner pizzeria. Always, only one man in
it. Hebrew gravestone cutter [pulleys, marble, smoke,
script not European]. Ice-cream vendor [closed for th'
winter]. Yesterday climbing up on bar stool next ex-
friend Agathe. Ordering drink + laughing: —*Does not th'
lord help them who help themselves?* Segueing [encore] to
how family fleeing smallpox epidemic, ca. 1885. By canoe

from Lachine. Further offering to impress: —*Sliding by Batoche*♥ near where baby Grandpa squeezing out, ca. 1900. Agathe, tight knit dress, good bangs, eyes round + green as aforementioned cat Etta's. Watching cette Anglaise's wrist waving limply West. Indicating family covering most of continent [in whatever conveyance]. Decade after decade. —*Limp as the tale I tiring of already*, thinking Agathe. Meaning, I/R ordering new round of shooters. And beer. Curls carefully pushed back. Smirking like everyone in this place at scratchy gangster voice on bar radio. Saying in this town a person buying anything: dope, bishops, cops, politicians. At top of bar mirror, blue LED: *Girls after high school, right on your monitor, taking off tight little panties + showing tight little...* appearing. Disappearing. Woman two stools down yelling meeting someone HARD. Especially if over 39! Were we not all eternally that? Thus bedding down with Good Vibrations? So

---

♥ What's in a name? Suffice to describe the site [complete with federal museum] on stunning rare natural prairie at curve of lovely river. Alive with flowers, insects, perfume, nurtured by ichor of final Métis stand against British crown. Red hawks flying over: battles are not lost forever. A priest in farther North Prince Albert, noting all the intermarriages between Aboriginal + European parishioners, blogs enthusiastically: *Here the Métis are legion, are winning!*

X, stop pretending to ask. Your small smirk behind your raised hand. Knowing full well R tale not about love. For a story, to be feasible, must be moving forward. Which is why I/R daily boarding avatar of public transport. Yesterday or before, #97 East. Corner boul Saint, old man, blue tattooed number on wrist, sitting down beside. Corner Mentana, anorexic 40s-style polka-dot nearly to stilettos tragic painted face of great ex-beauty. Corner Martyr-Dennis [which saint famous for walking out of Paris carrying his head], drunk, no ticket, pants sliding down. Smiling apologetically, wanting to be helpful, falling to knees to retrieve lady's glove. Bus writhing forth. When, out bus window, corner Drolet, déjà vu of dream where avenue on fire, smoke billowing black in Economical Footwear [silhouetted yellow-slicked firemen high-stepping o'er melting plastic shoes]. Billowing round soup-can pyramid in adjacent dépanneur. Sifting o'er red-tulled leather-harnessed torso in Jouets Joussifs window. Th' yellow cop tape over entrance preventing I/R from entering. To purchase little sexy videos + whatnots. For back in Room's dark end. Where

Ca 3:45p, winter light still leaking. Through the stained venetians. Glancing off ice-clad maple. Screechy school-yard on diagonal. Rumour of boots slipping on glassy outside stairs. Funerary scrape of shovel on icy sidewalk. And venetians raised a little, so *Face* now pressed on pane. Which *Face*, simultaneously — Reader, is not this the crux of our mystery? — ducking past keyhole-gaze of old Parisian. Toward darker half of railway-flat double. Silent + awkward as the apartment in *Dial M for Murder*. Notwithstanding it is difficult to hear.

The air is full of ~~cell~~ telephone.

Seven steps down, curled in tense ball to keep from falling off black paint-chipped perch, the resultant knot in the assistant's intestines perpetuating painful ferment of steamy pickled cabbage from Montréal Pool Room lunch. While his sluggish fingers dreaming code for importing words from squashed soccer-ball monitor on other side of Room wall. When, abruptly. With distant but pernicious rumble. The opposition between hidden + manifest fading. Plus all inhibitions. And Jean-François Jean letting go noisy rush of mephitic air. Concomitant with Command Failure fading on purple monitor to

> BED. With dark embroidery throw flanking end of the room. While on Grandma's platerail, tiny fly dancing little jig. Flying in the face of Peeet, the womanizer Baptist-Catholic. With space between his teee(t). That sentimental song's playing on the radio. Possibly revealing certain sexual practices. Who hath not dreamed of the sex of a hermaphrodite? ... Let's let

what Aunt Violet called the skeletons bleed. Out closet door. Like she let the tagged deer tongue pop out the dead deer mouth after some hunter pretending he'd shot her deer when she left it lying there a minute. And tagging its foot with his very own ticket. Now ... Violet, who at 15 sat Uncle Ef's kids. Fell. Pregnant when his wife died. Now ... was the way Grandpa started a story. NOW, his accent Western + confident. And we could smell the freshness of early morning. Stretching out behind the bathroom. His baking-powder toothpaste. Grandma no, he is cooking venison steaks + pancakes on polished wood stove. While you-know-who springing up + down in Veeera's amniotic fluid. Inches above sofa embroidery throw. We — though he held us upside down with our dress above our head like you hold a baby kitten to see what its sex is — had a happy childhood . . . .

The Fly [Resurgam!]

I/th' fly, havin' dozed a smidgen in upper stairwell reaches. To lullaby♥ of Fleur-de-lys, Sun-of-British-Empire, faux-

---

♥A nice Pilgrim lady happening in woods upon an Indigenous woman attaching her baby's cradle to a branch to rock in the breeze going home + penning: Rock-a-bye baby/In the treetop/When the wind blows/The cradle will rock/When the bough breaks/The cradle will fall/And down will go babyy/Cradle + all.vblows/The cradle will rock/When the bough breaks/The cradle will fall/And down will go baby/Cradle + all.

Goth cornices. Resonant with sweetly dissonant architectural playback. A music as beautiful, archaic, as music of th' spheres. Risin' + fallin' like ghosts in th' telephone. Chatterin' their intrinsic differentials. Fadin' with storm-flickerin' electric current. Abruptly reawakenin' to lights, action. Grammar of mid-life women, th' most unloved demographic. Callin' in to Celia Raw Raw©, lovin'ly advisin': Ceel, you're sick; you need custard, chicken soup. *Ceel asking a caller: Is it a good year for food?* Caller: *Yeah, always a good year for food. We're still eatin'!* Th' ~~furniture~~ background music breathin' down hall. Dark in th' centre, bright at th' extremities, like all flats in 'hood. Projectin', in coquettish sideways glancin's. Th' unconscionable connivin's + glimmerin' mahogany of apartment in *Dial M for Murder*. Simultaneously hearin' freezin' rain startin' to seriously batter roof. I/th' fly enjambin', for comfort, old gendarme's regulation Paris collar — bit of irregulation blue silk peekin' underneath [*always some body dividin' loyalties!*]. Essayin' a little hocus-pokey. To rain becomin' ice on contact with tar + gravel over. Accompanied, sub rosa, by mezzos moanin' from decades a' crackin' plaster fissures. Not to mention contemporaneous neighbourin' citizen dialectic ... —*I'll bash your head against the wall, that'll cure you of lovin' (me)* ... Then Celia, fortissimo, on radio, tellin' Indigenous comic great-great-grandma likely also Native. —*Must've been the blankets,* Indigenous comic crackin'. Addin' acerbic: *Is not the hybrid a melancholic? On a line between appearing + disappearing?*

All quiet a sec ...

Then, staccato claque of passer. Rushin' home to din-din. Footstep eager cause crotch quietly a-hardenin'. Thinkin' of little apéritif couple ritual: Him: —*Mmmm, babe, you smell delicious.* Her: —*Oh darling! But only if interruptus, promise!* Him, already lowerin' her on sofa. And nuzzlin' through openin' in bathrobe, th' lips, so instantaneously wet, he nearly slippin' in: —*Oops! Chérie, sorry; I'm really hot.* Her: —*Wait, wait, I haven't got my di ... Mmmm. Nice ... O! Okay! But only a minute, O! O!;* Him: —Oké doll, oops, sorry, gotta, gotta, gotta pull. She: —*Oh darling wait WAIT amin ...* Him: —Bébé I gotta ... She: —*WAIT, squeezin' hard.* They: —*Oh! Oh! Oh!* Which passer, in passim, glancin' up [for purchase] at *Face* in upper casement. Imaginin' woman's pear-shaped contours. Wigglin' on bed. In Room's dark end, bricked-in ca. 1950 for heatin' purposes. Th' oil company men still puffin' post-millennium up narrow back-shed steps. Heavy nozzle high for insertin' in leanin' tank behind dusty yellow kitchen. Itself openin' on aforementioned murky hall. In turn openin' on Room. Where *Face:*

That uncontrollable contingency, once more streaking past keyhole. Ancilliarily coated in same dusky, near-horizontal, light penetrating inner stairway. Via bottom oeil-de-boeuf door. Rendering our surveillants as splotches of miasma in corrupted stairwell air. Nitrogen. Methane. Ammonia from stagiaire J-F Jean's steamy hotdog lunch. Dust mites. Scatter neurons. Dead ketones. Whorling swarms + electrons. Odour o' p-p-p-patchouli from neighbouring sex-trade worker. On whose scarlet salon wall hookers in blouses, long skirts, wooden trunks held over heads, themselves on way out West, ca. 1910. Crossing rocky stream in little boots. Walking walking toward red disc of a timepiece perched atop a craggy peak. The peaks are purchases. The girls forever trucking. Occasionally regretting their cozy stained Saint-Jean-Baptiste quarter alcoves. Cheap velveteen draped o'er peeling plaster. Couches plumped + scented, for receiving quarry foremen, lower constabulary, tradesmen. But never on a Sunday, when out with their sweethearts, th' Shale Pit Workers! Youthful muscled arms holding soft girls tight in sweet night hay of carriage house + singing:

> *Les chairs me tremblent*
> *I've got th' shakes*
> *Elles peuvent ben me trembler*

And no wonder
L'hiver commence
Winter's comin'
J'ai tout bu mon été
I've drunk away my summer
O! verse, O! verse
Oh pour me another
Une chopine de whiskey
A nice drink of whiskey
Si j'fais une bonn' semaine
If I have a good week
J't paierai samedi
I'll pay you next Saturday...

Hélas, one hot June-wind night, alleged spark from cigarette catching hay in carriage house. And spreading to Crystal Palace's wooden walls, which in departing from pure glass-+-iron mother-country model meaning Palace instantaneously burning. To ground. But time [acumen] going its way. And ashy Palace gardens soon sprouting signboards lauding future most desirable quartier de Montréal. Was not air flowing fresh from mountain? Were not the new triplex flats boasting every early century convenience? Notably direct private access, regardless of level, to exterior. So Slavs. Anglos. Francos. Jews.

Portuguese. Greeks. Climbing decade after decade. Up iron stairs rattling ever louder under clomp of increasingly well-fed professionals. Doctors. Professors. Lawyers. State-radio reporters. While in margin of perception, 'neath yonder mountain two blocks South, vague murmurs of ice-fogged homeless voices in gloaming. Melding with moans of whining increasingly ice-coated branches. Shadow-bobbing o'er snow. And right through casements on to Settler-Nun walls. Like powdered wigs in a court. Are we not all prostheses? Moulded by circumstantial evidence?

*

How silent it is. I/Rosine lamey down to sleep. On dusty kitchen radio female voice bringing us th' weather. Boy is she ever. In Chibougamau, Trois-Pistoles, Chicoutimi, Jardins des Métis, Kuujjuaq, Sept-Îles, Témiscamingue, Abitibi, Matapédia. Another untimely storm signalling th' coming entertainment: Environmental Disaster. Always somethin' to complain. Not to be yielding to our time. As part of th' better-lawns crowd.

We lay-us down to sleep. Prayin' soul. To keep. Knowin' down th' blocks of Settler-Nun + o'er Mont-Royàl then o'er th' stretch of common blowin' yellow leaves. Marked

Ger-Many. Ko-so-vo [said que-ça-vaut]. Eeeeeeeeeeeeeas' Teeem. Or. If awake. Prayin' soul to take. Is not shame th' guilty fruit of Defeea[t]? Indig-nation? —*Only a quarter*, Uncle Peee[t] sayin'. But we are moulded by circumstantial evidence, so for th' future [+ R future tale within it], no visible dénouement. Still, she's movin'! Lovely wide cunt with wiry tuft wigglin' back + forth in préalable to gettin' hot. I am loath to go farther. Havin' to remain separate + different. Till everything is over. That could take forever. Even our flatulent assistant, sensin' little relish left, noddin' off, decountenanced.

How quiet it is. Through th' casement, th' swirling light from atop that cross-shaped building near th' bottom of th' city. Illuminating street, window, th' bridge of R nose. Cut like a diamond, like everyone's in th' family. Yes. It counts how you tell a story. Sherwood Forest + politicians having taught us th' significance of venetians. A little light dispersed, so that after somehow same as before. X, my inimitable betrayer, whose eyes're still somewhere spraying sunbeams + golden sparklers on sills. Will not R story, still, in th' way of sundials, be calibrating [mostly] sunny hours?

[Neighbour's Cut]   **The Street**

[NEIHB: She worked on the police desk. It made me
nervous. Admittedly, the parquet floors, she kept nice.
Also, she slept with women, a point in her favour. I thought
initially. I accepted to talk politics. But something was not
according to Hoyle. A wasp in a Frenchy sweater cannot
be trusted. Not in this place. I said, have you noticed a
Marxist does not invest in futures? To test her. The rental
property was for until Dacha Tranquillité, my little
organic farm, grew feasible. The orchard was maturing. I
said, wanting to be civil, you're a little back with the rent.
She answered, fingering the ivory spiral pendant hanging
from her neck, did I know Louis Riel'd♥ lived in the 'hood?
Lena with the cheekbones, on the second, a better tenant,
was complaining. The weird vibrations coming from over
woke her. I wrote a letter. You should have seen what airs

♥ What's in a name if perpetually under reconstruction by guilty opportunists?
Riel, French/Dene, hanged by Canada for starting a republican-style
revolution, himself proffering myth as a bulwark against future historicism
by adding Hebrew ascendance to the ancestral stew. Or so our protagonist
hearing from her mother, Veeera, who heard it from her mother, the Métis
Prisc Daoust, who declaring while serving the Sunday roast, using her
Coronation-pattern sterling, that Louis Riel was the reincarnation of David.
She read it in the paper.

Ms. 4-9-9-9 put on then. Like she was onstage. Flouncing down the stairs, striped top, you could peel it, workboots + stockings. Always different, from one day to the next. Like a girl. Like a boy. After she left the police desk at the paper — to put it better, after the police desk left her, A MULLET! I cannot tell a lie.]

STREET: In another frame, down street [elaborate white-painted wrought iron round exquisite tiled garden]: ~~birds~~ leaves begin falling. Man clenching fists in window. Face, arched nose, sensitive lips, swollen with anger + frustration. We had thousands of books. They burned them, saying why don't you Ay-rabs ever learn a thing? A tear running down cheek. Thinking of his father. He had huge culture + education + worked in a laundry. We've been here a hundred years. Man's face so swollen you can see heat coming off him. His kids, we are lumpen. Sitting at his desk, writing dots + circles in graceful right-to-left script. Weeping now fully.

[NEIGHB: I said to Jacko, put a carpet to drown the racket. She's driving Lena on the second sleepless! Plus send a letter. I need the rent for the dacha. In the orchard, the fruit, instead of falling, is ripening on the branches. Around it growing oats, to feed the rabbits. The day she answered the door, head to toe in leather, studs around her neck, my teeth — I caught a glimpse reflected in the leaded oeil-de-boeuf portal, a nice touch by Jacko before he left, which was fine with me — my TEETH were black with malice. She laughed + said: —*Never judge a book by its cover*. A voice also laughed behind. Lena, clean, nice with the children, told me there was screaming with pleasure every night. When you knew there hardly came a soul. People here are tolerant. But that girl was a sneak. She drilled a hole in the floor. Over Lena's bed. God alone knew why.]

STREET: There had been some rain. People having voted, scurrying over wet pocks in sidewalk, or jostling mid Épicerie Directe's air-conditioned crowded fruit. On th' radio, ridings going right. Kamouraska-Temiscouata. Dubuc. Matane. Woman, in paying, hoisting bum on brown grocery counter, fingering curls of handsome boy cashier. —*Moi*, she saying. *And Mother before me. We always worked for th' unions. Th' Independence Party. Th' French language.* —*Euh, excewse* [I/Rosine interjecting] *euh, puis-je payer?* Th' woman, dark hair, slim pants, crossed at th' knees, nice heeled boots, in English: —*Oh, from your accent, you're Cana-dienne. I don't blame you. For what you do. But we Québécois, we've been fighting for centuries.* I/R: —*J'ai voté Solidaire!* Woman: —*Moi, I'm strictly indépendantiste, but if Canadienne like you ...* I/R [angry]: — *I'm

59

more Autochtone [exaggerating peut-être]. *Than anything!*
Woman: — *Oh? Me too, ¾ Abenaki. You Mohawk?* I/R
shaking head. We walking out together. Woman, turning
East on Dada-Jesus. *Ogigawi! Goodbye!* Only word learned
from Grandfather.

[NEIGHB: I told the shrink MacBeth:
    Can you believe she stole the salt bag?
    Like Miss Environment protects the lilacs?
    I said, what makes girls like you tick?
    Oh she said, I hear it makes you retch ...]

STREET: In hotel foyer. One block over. Hot October.
I/Rosine passing *Free Khalid X* flyers. For th' principle [+
small remuneration]. Th' air conditioning. Refreshing for a
minute. Professors milling at cocktail table. Cuban with no
future in R story, coming up + saying: —*Cuban-American.
No, -Canadian, he amending. I liked what you saying in your
futuristic pamphlet. So oh-penn Give me your e-mail.* Writ
in little book with flurry of CIA agent, he walking away,
grey tufts of hair flying about large beige ears. Meaning
now they've got me in their system. Autrement dit, as one
orgasm producing another [on dark satin sheet, her wide
ass switching back + forth, suspect as th' colour beige].
So one cliché, etc., till every Cuban a spy. In *my* defence:
was not I/Rosine Dousse a small smooth woman arriving

from Haeckville, AB? Via Grandpa's friend madame B's in border town of S-D? And getting in initially with group, designated DANGEROUS by Fed. Gov. Ag. For whom any info, when requested under Freedom of Information Act, forwarded nearly totally felt-pen redacted. As per para 7a in legislation wherein any gov. inst. refusing to give access to a rec. requested under Act, shall state: *This rec. does not exist.*

[NEIGHB: I said, Jacko, we need a lawyer. Relax, he told me as he exited. Going down substantially in my estimation, he hit the road for Toronto. Like he knew already the place was going up in flames.]

STREET: Speaking of flames, the other day, I/R boarding #55 North. In slanty light from port. Having once more started for but failing to reach Lachine.♥ Th' chauffeur,

---

♥ We materialists [like paranoids] know facts speak for themselves. *Fact:* Explorers early seeking Northwest passage to la Chine find waters permanently frozen. *Fact*: The town, mockingly named Lachine after explorer seeking, somewhat later, *inland* China passage, soon becoming main site of embarkation for fur-company voyageurs paddling toward lustre sun in West. *Fact*: Business is booming. Decade after decade *Fact*: Business keeps booming. Sun, ever brighter, thanks to CO_2 from now industry's interminable advance, slowly thawing far North passage, opening possible shipping route to China. Mission accomplished!

usual French + Irish mix, curly caramel goatee, refusing to converse. Listening to les Canadiens on radio. SHOOTING not scoring. Waves of *awhhwahwahhhh* coming up from dashboard. Meaning I/R, curling in front corner seat. Dark silk shirt, spiky cock-ring on wrist [grant it, a little passé in fashion]. And delivering opinion re: les chauffeurs de la STCUM. Un syndicat supposément au service du peuple. For failing to adumbrate or sing little songs. Save for chauffeur of #80, av. du Parc. Who at all times crooning show tunes for passengers: 'Ohhhhh, What a Beautiful Mornin',' 'We Could Have Danced All Night,' 'Bâââli Haaaa'ii...' But on this particular day. #55 North, wheezing up boul Saint. Passing, on occasion, buildings on fire. Meaning I/R, who having too often kept mum, because yielding to her time, therefore knowing th' importance of informants. Vowing to look, before afternoon expiring, into all th' little glass doors of all those fire-alarm box installations. Courtesy Les Terroristes Urbains. On corner poles up + down the street. Which little red boxes contemporaneously channelling not telegraph alarms to fire stations, but dioramas of burning boul Saint buildings yesterday or tomorrow. Built with stone hoisted from Saint-Jean-Baptiste quarries by th' Shale Pit Workers! Themselves smoking in little appliquéed diorama insets:

Firebox 1, corner Sainte-Cat: Diorama of already torched beaux-arts porn cinema façade. Grainy charred pretty legs of women.

Firebox 2, corner Of-Pines: Falafel resto façade. Tagged 'Burning Tomorrow.' Gape-holed sinking onion turret high over. Aswarm with enterprising pigeons. Cooing. Fucking. Shitting on scare-owl's realistic feather detail.

Firebox 3, Bagg or Napoléon: French revival dormers o'er Kiki's Shoes [not always in matching pairs] + battered oak chamfered door. To be 'Burning next week.'

Firebox 4, corner Rachel: Singed Nouveau Monde Antiques card in smoky diorama window. Offering original Riel script claiming Indians of continent descendants of ancient Hebrews of Egypt.

Firebox 5, angle New-City: Mile-End vernacular [curvy cornerstone balcony], housing hotdog vendor famous, ca. 1930, for sticking finger in lieu of wiener into bun. Ere dribbling mustard + wrapping. Surreptitiously withdrawing manus particulari. Meaning some hungry mid-depression rag-trade seamstress slushing down sidewalk. Thinking she lost it. What's a girl to do? Pretend still back in Macedonia. And keep moving!

Bus grinding North, passing frail town-bred trees. Pale amber branches now that winter approaching, pluming toward sky. Or is that smoke on th' rise? Lengthening toward already sooty potlid of clouds. Spied through filthy bus window. Then one more red fire-alarm box object. Mid bakery display of aging ramekins. Loaves. Cheese rolls. Bagels. Palmiers. So jumping up + ringing bell. I rang. And rang. And rang. —*Merci, madame*, sneering caramel-bearded driver. Braking hard, th' better to project this faithful STCUM user toward bakery display window, featuring in middle, no firebox installation: only square of red bond paper. With poem in unofficial language:

It is with sadness we must announce the closing of
St. Lawrence Bakery
We thank our many loyal customers, retail
and wholesale
Who have remained with us and
Who have appreciated our bread, danish
and pastry products
Where the technology was primarily our
minds and hands
Thank you. Thank you very much.

Smoke toujours on rise. I/R, though loath to give in to her time as part of th' better-lawns crowd. Having escaped to

Mile-End, QC, from Haeckville, AB, via Catholic College in S-D. In search of th' action. Still, wanting, a priori, to get to safe confines of Settler-Nun Room. Miraculously succeeding hailing a Taxi Aimable. Wherein, for reasons of efficiency, coyly resisting mentioning allusions from Les Terroristes Urbains re: origin o' conflagrations. Only joking to chauffeur: —*Pretend we're in Macedonia. And keep moving.* Which chauffeur, anyway, accommodatingly nosing, Catholic moustache in mirror. Lithely as vehicles on a freeway in + out of gridlock. Abruptly hitting smoke-free pocket. By unscathed blind brick façade of Sam's Superior Steaks. Substantial bouncer in film-noir livery laissant passer exquisite mink lady. Accompanied by sleek dude suit, sporting L-for-Liberal-shaped diamond clip. Sparkling ostentatiously in sudden rewind sequence to sur-real scene of very same Superior Steaks door. Swinging open on precisely same Superior Steaks stairs, partly visible through slightly ajar entry. Back in the day when there was still an afternoon edition. And I/R, police reporter, entering. Cool French suit:

+[dude, eating steak]

+[liver]

+[dude saying he knowing who putting
Pierre Laporte, Labour Minister, ca. 1970,
in trunk]

+[did she want to write about it for her rag?]
-[she, feeling afraid, saying but I then only 10!

= CABBIE SETTING MADAME STRAIGHT:

—Madame, mon père le boucher took me once for dinner. We marched straight back to la chambre froide. Instead of nice red meat, c'était all strung up with côtes turning blue! Mon fils, Papa said, c'est comme ça qu'on a le meilleur steak en ville. Môman, I never saw him so happy…

At that very moment th' overconnectedness of experience fundamental to th' paranoia any citizen by definition usually trying to deflect. Gesticulating + honking, to get away from th' fire. Catapulting chaotically up smoky boul Saint causing I/R's mouth in rear-view mirror to be urging cabbie to go faster. Faster. Adding, perhaps mysteriously: — *Th' better to avoid th' enemies of th' planet. Whose number are legion.* Knowing that tow-headed ground-floor Potter. At this time of day, stepping out with Chocolate Latte. Depositing pale stools beneath th' lilacs. Which Potter, on seeing I/Rosine Dousse pulling up in taxi: gliding back astonished. As if I/R some kind of revenant opening taxi door. Head high. Curls, temporarily bleached, somewhat resembling — Auntie Dill always saying — Princess Grace of Monaco. Albeit lacking adequate self-esteem. So th' Potter's mock-shocked look meaning trying even harder to be very very friendly. In interest of neighbourly relations. Laughing. Joking. Balancing on one foot. Then t'other. Lovely derrière step by step retreating. Backwards, up embarrassingly creaky outer stairs. Only on opening second gallery door + entering murky stairway, full of smelly splotches + miasma — only then registering that th' Potter. Having waved Rosie off unfavourably.

VENETIANS THAT EVEN PRIVATE
EYES HAVE TROUBLE SLEUTHING

Now we do th' can-can. On Grandma's plate rail. To tell th' truh(t). I can hear 'em saying No Girl Wert'er Salt'd have a fly as Nar-Râteur. Unless she lacked teeet[h]! Grandpa's clack into place. Here is a clou in th' case. Rosine, R future in-tra-la-la-di-ê-ge-tic Nar-Râtrice's standing half-naked on a painting talking to a skeleton. So tis the reek of death that horrid insect delects? Or family compound air? Leaking amniotic fluid? Grandpa sweating? Sockies? Splayed? Excess [th' family reeked of sex]! Secrets? To be possibly revealed. No, keep it hidden, sayin' Grandpa to th' little princess sittin' on his right. Referrin' to th' Easter basket. Or your brothers will eat 'em up. She wears her salmon-coloured dress with th' striped gussets up side. Smilin' up at him under albino curls, she wiggles her little tail, sayin' *Grandpa, I'm a fis'*. Grandpa's brown watchmaker's hands, rollin' excellent tobacco, disappear at the diamond-studded cuff into fresh linen. He glances in his teacup. Where he can see th' future. His little granddaughter with long shiny eyes + gold-white ringlets. Is ridin' on a bus. He addresses th' company: *R child will be sent to Christian college in San Diego* . . . .

The Empty Middle

Earlier this morning, I/R drinking first cup of coffee, taste fogged with usual toxins. Th' less you delect, th' more impercipient th' grinding, rimming, tight screw + bubble. On radio Celia Raw Raw© announcing Leonard: King of Montréal artists. Oh MAN what a 70s. Frankly I was lounging. In th' shade of greeny half-light denoting Mile-End to th' familiars. When two ladies formerly of this place [poudrées, peintes, parées]. Having migrated, ca. 1960, from dark-in-th'-middle [but bright-at-th'-extremities!] 4999 Settler-Nun flat. To newer white iridescent brick Saint-Luke's Rise. Nostalgically wanting to come up. Meaning I/R slamming bottom stairway door. Though dying to ask if inner railway-flat Room always this ugly stucco? Was not my day unfolding luxuriously as predicted? Contemplating th' oscillating Octoberish/ November elements. And serenely not caring futurity as yet offering no key to dénouement. Th' slant of light via silver-grey venetians. Simultaneous with single bird call high in ice-shorn maple. Not to mention th' lucite air of morning, rendering air so transparent. A little haze dispersed. Small ha ha's t'auras ta souris. Occasionally emitting from dark half-forgotten alcoves. Me, on th' bed, singing in high prose voice —*Darling, you have broken my heart.* Knowing full well one does not in forward-moving chronicles. Propulsed by th' telephone, th' radio, th' bus, th' aeroplane, th' digital. Themselves saturated with longing. Dwell upon love. Yet: *IF* singing, then *NOT* glancing back, like what's-his-name leaving Hades, obsessive glint in eye, at yellowed pages of th' *Book of Genocides.* Earlier tossed from open casement in memoriam of Veeera's ancestors. Chased by squatters who ever after guiltily expecting catastrophe at any moment, unto the third + fourth generation. Only, in lying down again, I/R failing to abide. Upon love's beautiful [if melancholic] heights. Slipping back, instead, to that terrible afternoon in Hotel Stella, somewhere on prairie, where you, X, you insatiable bitch, having fucked yourself all th' way from Haeckville, AB [one hand on wheel]. Smashing hotel glass table, your bloody fingers playfully wiggling. Toward I/R's perfect throat, conveniently in situ in aperture of hotel bathroom door. Which throat opening + whispering for us to laugh some more:

    —You said you packed your gloves.

Far from recountin' all we know in that domain, I/th' fly restrictin' my observations to earlier this mornin'. R Surrogate sippin' coffee in railway-flat middle. Th' shade of half-drawn venetians striatin' her caramel skin under off-shoulder vintage pink moire bathrobe. Was not th' blonde in *Dial M for Murder* likewise breakfastin' in pink [discreetly pearled at neck]? Her raised cheatin' eyebrow readin' in mornin' paper th' lover's ship arrivin'. While on yellow kitchen radio Celia warnin' re: comin' ice storm. 'Makin' highway like any rink in th' country.' Meanin' Rosie, when openin' middle gallery door, likely not runnin' into Neighbour [aka th' landlord]. Descendin' from veggie-powered vehicle + morphin', on hearin' small bird singin' high in tree, into wondrous chin-raised posture of maid in Northern forest. Ere, in crossin' court to collect th' rent, likely scopin' pages torn from *Book of Genocides*. Scuttlin' o'er macadam. But first R usual second pot of espresso. Followed by usual complex ablutions. Hair. Foundation.Plus pennin' little ode to make you, X, you proto-assassin, jealous:

> *Had a lover*
> *With big equipment*
> *How I*
> *Miss her*

Promptin' hasty la-di-da retreat to Room's dark end. Bendin' low past keyhole, toujours rife with incontinent gaze of ancient Parisian. Who, notwithstandin' need for a pipe + a pipi, maintainin' shoulders thin as a skeleton's in

Eureka position. Ignorin' th' dancey musca feet [turnout th' envy of Nureyev] essayin' little samba on back of old cop's decayin' neck: I/th' fly stickin' backside out + swivellin' to left, pirhouettin' to right. Bendin' one knee, then t'other, tappin feet, adamant. When inconsiderately swept by bony gendarme finger—*pas-de-deuxin'* into ether. Flickin' my posterior to click-click of radiator. Ere shimmyin' down ray pene-tratin' oeil-de-boeuf portal. And landin' precisely back on cuttin' edge of spotty Paris-laundered ancient gendarme collar. *Fritti-frottin'* a little. Limitin' my responsibility to certain sensations electives.

There is definitely a body!

Lest in funeral pall of light, tis only th' fishy stench of c__♥ R Surrogate projectin'. Th' shiny spot on smooth inner thigh, typical of girls' thighs in grassy regions. Akimbo on bed. Still, she's movin'! Raisin' baby finger. Ah, that small baby finger, conic, diminutive, capable of

---

♥ Further re: names: What better term than 'c__' to name the famous gap between body + sign? For 'c__,' unlike male homologue, 'normally' configured indirectly. Take J. Doucet's *Dirty Plotte* comic about the 'first' Québécoise woman astronaut. Whose well-groomed Québécoise mother, scarf expertly tied, arriving on launch pad, very last minute. Proffering box of cookies with rough oatmeal edges that the astronaut(e), beginning to orbit, is rubbing on her clit. Mmmm. Good..., she's writing to Maman. Need we add that in Québécois 'plotte' means 'c___'? So the series, read as 'dirty plot' in English, really meaning 'dirty c__'!

absorbin' vibrations unavailable to larger A-type pinkies. Th' tinklin' of ~~silver spoons at Grandpa~~'s ice-cycles about to fall from sheds. Night cracklin' o'er frozen macadam of court, itself laid o'er gravel. Laid o'er cement. Laid o'er packed earth, under which rottin' pilons of burnt-down Crystal Palace. Still emittin' their acridity:

—*But some saying Palace built on raft!*

—Impossible! *With our galleries, ca. 1880, bearin' weight of British Colonial Artillery Drillers' guns. Plus, when velocipedes, 'them old bone-shakers,' iron-tired, came in. People ridin' there. While on Palace grounds those Shale Pit Workers! so proud + strong. Gatherin' for sport.*

—*Even during the smallpox epidemy, countless bubble faces subsiding daily in those hospices set up in dairy. Stables. Granary. Those still standing, men of courage, tearing notices warning of PICOTTE!*♥ *On one day alone [I read it in the paper]: 18 avis announcing dead or dying ripped down. One on Sacred-Refuge, two, rue Martyr-Dennis, six, rue Brothers-Dominican, four, boul Saint, three, ruelle Heavenly-Mirage.*

♥ No translation required. The onomatopoeia of *PICOTTE* (standard Fr: variole) struck fear into waking consciousness of all Montrealers, though the deaths mostly happening in poorer French quarter of Saint-Jean-Baptiste, inhabited by Shale Pit Workers! Which quarter under sway — crowing the anglo media — of anti-inoculation priests. While the French papers daily, sadly, recording the number of *picotte* deaths per street.

Pale *Face* peeps out.

In the movie, was not the elegant blonde future Princess Grace of Monaco leaving unclassy peeping to illicit secret lover, the besotted mystery-novel author? And to Scotland Yard detective [combing his moustache]? Simultaneously peeping between barely parted curtains, earlier drawn neat + tight by hubby, now scoped coming up walk toward a disastrous dénouement. While th' classy blonde wife, focused, defined in sober teal dress tailored over small padded breasts. Scoping his arrest demurely from pénombre. Notwithstanding herself having done time for murdering used-car salesman, abruptly walking immaculate out of prison. No longer guilty. Into arms of #2 man.

Telephone ringing.

Blonde head turning.

Phone ringing again.

To little Rosine in dark red Princess Theatre of Haeckville, AB, marquee of square black vertical letters, nice lights around it, running down the false front of stucco building, the best part: the Hot Buttered Popcorn. The phone on the lamb-bent screen ringing, ringing. The beautiful head of actress, blonde + curled under [like Veeera doing hers that very morning]. Turning, turning. Because somebody maybe wanting to kill her. After the popcorn was finished, the blonde future princess. Instead of dying as planned, herself stabbing hit man with scissors. Who drove a secondhand car. Which was too bad for him, thinking Rosie. Walking home with little cousin B, who looks like an Indian. [Which comment earning soft cuff from Veeera's skinny hand.] And albino cousin N. In dim November light. Blue firs, black in the dusk. Brown clapboard houses.

A dead blonde lynx in back of a truck.

And Rosie. Walking with the two most beautiful cousins in the world. Black-brown. And white-white. Not really understanding why the man in the movie kept phoning back his wife. If he was really Diming Her for Murder. Diming was what hurt Grandpa most. When someone tried to bargain an already break-the-bank price for a very fine die-mond. Walking. Her little head was, however, mostly full of red movie-theatre upholstery. Plush as in Princess Margaret's picture in Grandpa's kitchen. Ermine trim. Magenta cape. Tiara. Rubies. Seed pearls fresh as dew on th' grass. Or swarming in moving permutations + combinations o'er th' mountainous expanse of Dill's [pink] sweater. Advancing in wheelchair o'er highway in Kelowna. Slingbacked foot stuck out aggressively. In front. To warn off th' traffic.

Ca. 4:15p. *Face* looking down on court. And seeing no ~~mandate~~ landlord, exiting middle gallery door. Sheepskin at dewpoint of uninteresting or expired [yet curly cuffs fashionably turned out]. Boarding #55 South, straight to back-end horizontal seat. And torquing to scope via rear bus window, th' icy black ribbon narrowing to sunset. Infinite as shining road curving up + o'er Castor River. In Notown, ON, where Papa Reeef 'movin'' 'em' awhile. When #29 Rachel East spattering #55 back pane. Not to mention *C'est-extra-dancing/French-jazzy-swing-avec/Cowboys-fringuants* rear-panel ad rolling into Saint-Urbane Cadet HQ stop. For trio of young bloods, shiny lenses avant, like soldiers in a march-pass. Hand-strapping down aisle. Bus, in slipping out again, scraping corner balcony protruding low o'er street. Fat kid, turning musically a-side. Abruptly pointing up —*There! Last summer, drinkin' beer. Sayin' he a terrorist.* IRA *tattooed in big fuckin' letters right across back. I went down with him to th' Dublin Pub. Guys there sayin' he afake. Got very mad, told him to prove it...*

Silence a minute. Boys swaying intently. Eyeing in corner of retina large tits. Ankles under flared pants. Salt-stained platforms + glossed mouths on side horizontal seats. Lip-synching in French. Portuguese. Créole, into cellphones. As word 'terrorist' ricocheting through stagnant bus air. Conjuring 'Tel Aviv' to fat kid. 'Young-Palestinian-shirt-blown-off-suicided-back' to skinny pointy-head beside. While I/R on back horizontal seat having deja vu of empty bottle suddenly last summer.

Projectiling from exact same illegally protruding balcony into likely same #55 South. Through open bus window. And grazing R little flowered dress. Stretched over knees. Sitting up straight on back horizontal seat. Always late, as usual. In hope-against-hope's royal light of dusk. On way to meeting you, my Magnolia. Later ~~face~~ fingers all bloody fucking. After Schwartz's pepper steak + liver. We also liking to stroll about. Dancing th' samba + speaking ~~Oxonian~~.

Fly [*encore*]

We phantoms in th extra Dia-Jeesis. Unrelated to love's object, therefore gettin' to keep th' one sense♥ uncon-nected to it. Seein' whole picture. *She's not there but here!* Her familiar sweet contours. Pear hips. Luscious yet not oversized breasts [oh to smell th' oysterish aroma of her] on black satin sheet. Watchin' tree branches, most thick. Near lamp in th' street. But some people needin' to be separate + different. Though th' heart screams: I want warmth, want breasts, want the slatchy-skatchy ivory smell of skin, want th whole creamy creamy embrace. O Hip —what are you doin'? Relaxin' buttocks a little, I/th' fly [knowin'

| ♥ 6th sense, of course.

th' value of retardment] openin' all my 100 orifices to ambient interferences: th' foggy icy rain. That homeless chick screechin' on macadam —*Bastard! Bastard! Bastard ...You Roy janitor, pretending to have the building! People! In hand! That is why your reference to eviction.* Not to mention guy dronin' on coast-to-coast-to-coast official state radio —*In this land everyone an immigrant.*♥ Then lightspot tap-tappin' pianissimo right through Room casement. O'er antique wash-stand. Broken turtle rattle. O'er th' three dark sisters [Veeera, Dill, Maddie] gazin' down from family portrait, signed Mott Photos of Haeckville, AB. And

Suddenly: they all comin' alive. Proud heads held high. Assimilated. Successful. Apart from th' supremely confident Grandpa, perhaps overemphasizin' appearance? One baby, head-back to camera. Starin' through lace curtains. At

---

♥ What leads generation after generation of new arrivals in the Americas to endlessly iterate that everyone here an immigrant? From earliest fresh-faced settler boys enlisting, for economic reasons, soon leaning over pits + bayonet-ting every copper skin that moved. Ere standing + hollering a song like in the musical Oklahoma! About the land being grand + belonging to us, a-yippie-i-o-ee-ay. Farther North, soldiers shooting 'when required'; otherwise, devi-ously kidnapping Aboriginal children into conditions that killing thousands [strangely, the word genocide refused]. Voices on state radio, though contem-poraneously acknowledging guilt, still regularly iterating old colonial mantra: *In-this-country-everyone-an-immigrant.*

light glintin' off old McLaughlin. Used for dusty liquor run from Fernie to Butte, MT. Always with revolver on seat. Grandpa himself, no gangster. But sometimes ridin' with brother Craie. A mechanic. Who, sayin' Peeet.— *Workin' for Picariello. Pic always hirin' mechanics. Th' danger not in drivin' th' McLaughlin chockfulla liquor south to Montana. But comin' back, with highway robbers chasin' for th' $$$$$. Craie, adding Pete, never getting caught. But Pic, whose cheese factory nothin' but a front, hanged for shootin' a Royal!* Does not th' lord help them who help themselves? Was not a family [Grandpa always sayin'] to gain respect: dressin' spiffily + contributin' to a local denomination?

Hélas, C-N's pantssss are wet. The regulation gendarme wool chafing ancient yet tendre thighs. Erstwhile Paris-laundered collar grievously impissated by mothy worsted uniform, growing sweatier + sweatier. Given uncharacter-istic inner stairway heater, placed too near drafty lower stairway door [for warming boots in winter]. Making ambience so soporific, old cop drifting, half-asleep, to rue Mouffetard, Paris, ca. 1924. Where already on fresh-bent knee, his young cadet peeking. Through large brass aper-ture or keyhole. Noting in minuscule carnet:

Floor made of thick square boards forming diamond pattern, popular ca. 1850, buildings constructed by our Parisian worker co-ops. Mantel [black], mirror trimmed in gold. Christmas-tree lights around it. Black velvet drapes held back with ribbon on casement window open on acacias in blossom. Subsequent tenants bending over, for reasons indisibles, likely mistaking stains on parquet for wine.

Old Casse-Noisette further taking dream-catcher feet, feather-shuffling on wall by current 4999 Settler-Nun bed, Mile-End, QC. For a second individual in 1924 chambre-de-bonne in Paris. Leaning low + whispering to figure on bed: —*A movable feast*. But cadet, being at end of his shift, already out rue Mouffetard door. Past domed Panthéon caption *Aux grands hommes la patrie reconnaissante*. O'er Pont-Neuf. ~~Mauve gloved hands~~. Toward Café Brecht, rue Belloc in 8me. Eager soft polished boots back-forthing o'er butt-spattered mosaic floor. Seeking l'ami canadien. Wanting to touch the silky skin beneath Jos.'s fine woven shirt, standing near bar. The Parisian cadet raising pillbox + snapping knotty fingers for round of triple sec. Ignoring that Jos.'s Hellenic profile aiming at pair of very female French wrists. In little black gloves on cafe's zinc bar counter. Jos, spreading with slender artisan fingers, the fold of animal-skin wallet. Full of tiny diamonds, emeralds, rubies, hesitatingly, slowly, caressingly, parting the lips of leather.

Dial M for Murder

4:30p: A dreadful loneliness penetrating stairway. The reigning air of denial combining, nisi prius, with decelerating ions. Ristling like insect feet on student hacker's negative-lit monitor. Himself presently devoting moment to hating progenitor. That tapette proprietor of Taxis Aimables. A wimpy sissy fake. Like all men over 50 raised by the priests. For sending him to police school. He, Jean-François Jean, young, theatrically gifted. Instinctively preferring his mononcle Pax Robichon. That bad actor, sa matante Agathe liking to joke. Pax, last seen on lunch break by l'École nationale de théâtre. Smoking une clope + affecting slight limp. White shirt, ring, bracelets, cross pendant with ruby set in. Likely for role of Rive-Sud thug. Muttering in one of those tough, half-whisper gangster voices:
I never killed.
My patron Robillard, oui.
Moi: chamais.
The stagiaire, like his uncle Pax, a romantic. But in the post-Goth way of those pubescent immediately

pre-millennium: wanting to play Ligéia. What could be more heavenly than E. Poe's dead Ligéia? Rising, black eyes flashing, victorious, from appropriated corpse of the anemic inconsequential replacement spouse. Rowena, her weak husband marrying too quickly. Rowena, so boring, the castle suffering from bedsores. Rowena, whose dying body Ligéia vampirizing completely. For purpose of reclaiming rightful place mid exquisite castle boudoir volutes of curtains. Of richest cloth of gold. Embossed at intervals with jet arabesque figures. About a foot in diameter. Young J-F finding her so lovely, he letting go a mammoth. Whose odour expanding right through door-panel crack into Room's dark end. Where a diaphanous foot on bed stamping. Stamping out voice yesterday yelling up from alley: —*Washing sex toys on balcony not nice for the children.* As if still in era of Victoria Regina. When on Crystal Palace lawns:

Hours passing in lovely summer picnics. Mid flora + fountains. Where Shale Pit Workers! washing feet + taking swigs. Singing they'll pay next week. Or wrestling, sleeves neatly rolled up. One arm tied back, as sketched in *La Patrie*. So strong + virile they capable of resisting dreaded smallpox virus. Though narrow Saint-Jean-Baptiste streets ringing with struggle. As soldiers in early dark imposing quarantine on humble walkups. Meaning some setting out, like early voyageurs, from Lachine. Perhaps sliding past beautiful Batoche on beautiful curve of river. On magnificent prairie. Shortly after ubiquitous British troops march-passing Métis houses. Jealously noting their quality. Cleanliness. Tables + chairs scrubbed with homemade lye soap. After every meal. And always several fiddles hanging on wall.

Smiling broadly, soldiers' freckled fingers preparing regulation torches.

Two Blocks Over, MacBeth

[Eyes incarnadine]. Peers out. At gas station. Hamburger joint. Faux-deco College Socrate [*Français, Anglais, Grecque, Italien, Arabique, Espagnol*]. Cement-block refugee hotel opposite. Latest crop of arrivals. Lounging in front.♥ It is autumn. The sidewalk blowing with yellow leaves from parc opposite. Globe in his hand. A client entering. Behind. Aubergine dye job typical of hags in the 'hood. Purse tight under arm. Settling imperiously in gently contoured École du meuble de Montréal leather-backed chair. He knew her father. A predator. A paranoid. Prodigious energy of shady entrepreneur. Who, after nombreuse famille asleep, slipping off to bathhouse establishment opposite Little Children of Jesus's Latino-inflected wedding-cake façade. With famous rare mid-façade statue of adolescent Jesus gazing straight over Little-Children-of-Jesus Square. Into steamy bathhouse

---

♥ What do authorities do with the unwanted? First they canton them in refugee covens found in Western cities. With cubicles whose 'walls' for reasons of aeration not quite up to ceiling, raising temperature in summer + general erotic ambience to sizzling. Thus, an artist of our acquaintance, tall, willowy, caught, one nice afternoon, en flagrant délit with handsome squeeze from somewhere in Africa. By younger local girl in taffeta, little rousse couettes, screaming over partition: *Lâche donc mon homme.*

windows. Whose recessed blue door endlessly opening to delectable youths strolling nonchalantly off street. Not to mention the rapid left-right-glance-step-glide of older married guys. The father, pockmarked like his infamous port-syndicate boss uncle Fred Ball, putatively linked with West-end mob. She's crossing her knees. Lax linen slacks [—*Go shopping, bitch!*]. Shoulders low, back. Hurling with the unselfconsciousness of the entitled:

—*If you could see what's going in + coming out!*

MacBeth sits. Unwashed hand, for anchorage, on École du meuble desk's substantial amber calf. Face blank due to orange backlight from window. She has thin but shapely lips [he has to admit]. Mouth part open. In speaking, never purses. Thus guarding softness of frontal contour. Tongue coming out when disgusted. Ugh — a fat thing. A rat.

—*Jo, I understand you want it nice when you retire from the farm. And come back here to live. Plus, you're mad at Jacko, who on a sunny day moved out + left you the trouble. Your heart is broken. It's your investment. Brother Conrad warned you about real estate.*

—*Washing sex toys on the balcony. Tub. Apron. Suds. Dildo like a stallion's!*

—Jo, maybe you have in common —

—I can get her out if I want. For now, I am tending my garden.

MacBeth glances round. At dirty avenue, under. In-grate, he thinking again. The only prime real estate facing airy Mont-Royàl opposite: chrome-+-plate-glass McRonald's. Giving way immediately to flat-topped, dated diners. Dépanneurs, Dairy Kings. Treetops of Our Lady of Snowy Angels cemetery. Rising beyond. Extending toward Shaar Hasho-mayim, whose peaceful fuchsia-flowered vistas meandering between rows of close-set stones, the most beautiful cemetery in city. Waiting for her to speak. Globe still in hand, MacBeth turning head. Tartly now in direction of alley. Where backs of stacked flats rectangularly framing three-sided skinny courts. Close. Promiscuous. Already at 6a this morning. One of those nosy upper-floor biddies, the one with the mouse in her purse. Watching him progressing down lane. Accompanying the incomparable lover from Flatbush. To bus. [Pause for revering boyfriend's scented dreads + cheeky butt, a dancer in fact.] The nosy parker in upper window screaming like supporting actress in some old Hitchcock thriller:

—There's going to be a doozer!

The client: —*So. I'm collecting for the food co-op—not to mention trying to squeeze some rent—she's answering the door, wiggling ass + provoking*: —Hey, you know Louis Riel, before you Anglos hanging, living five blocks over? *I loaned her my* Book of Genocides. *To show her. What I know. She tore it. Fortunately for her, not yet a collectible.*

Carefully he stands. Commemorating, with surreptitious pat, the cat-o'-nine-tails last night dexterously applied to ass. Anticipating [not to his credit] the laugh he'll have with Rosie. Eyeing, below, two handsome [i.e., skinny] ~~junkies~~ actors. Pencil-thin denims. Three days' growth. Nervy, so mean-when-unavoidable. Gesticulating too rapidly on filling-station bench. He waits. The fading red-orange autumn ray sneaking a sec through cloud. Powdering his baize-padded wall. He waits. Silence. Now the client's bringing up her grandmother. Born in bottom flat, at 4995 Settler-Nun, ca 1911. So you own it, he thinking bitterly. Intoning:—*You told me about her. Sitting on a chair in her kitchen. A paper in some script not quite, you insisting, European. Unfolding on flowered lap. Obviously covering some desire you, Jo, incapable of offering to yourself.*

The client, thumbs inverted, blurting:—*The tenant on the second, Lena, clean, nice to the children, had to tell one, skinny, heart-shaped glasses, making such a racket skipping non-stop up + down the stairs: Vamoose! The ground-floor Potter, coming herself from Portland, saying crystal meth for sure ...*

—*So?* escapes from his lips.

MacBeth sits gingerly. Noting in his book: *In the prolonged absence of the love object, the obsessive turns against her environment.* He sighs, trying to be nice:

—*You know, dear Jo, first impressions can be false. Be that as it may, a ~~tooth~~* [he means truth] *can sometimes get extracted. Remember how things went beautifully. After you at first moved. Leaving your flat to Ms. Dousse: the vacation. Fall. Winter. Holes, pimples, blackheads utterly forgotten. Already, from down the street. You were loving Rosine, your new tenant's curly little head. She was your replacement.*

—*You're crazy. Like my mother.*

He looks out again. Wondering why women suffer more from ruminations, anxieties, petty quarrels, fatigue + depression. *The soul that in life did not its divine right/ Acquire, has not even in Hades, repose.* In five, the phone will ring. Lover, calling from Flatbush, before going off to pick up his regular further out in Brooklyn: he loves him. MacBeth's finger, nail exceptionally not quite impeccable, being still perfumed with the hole of the other, swiping rapidly by nostril:

—*Jo, to think about this week: you, a gardener, are weeping over her silver bells, her cockle shells, her pretty maids. In a row.*

—*For this I am paying?*

—*I'd beg you, don't lean out the window. But with you, there's no danger.*

She likes it. Snapping purse + clasping under armpit. Green baize-padded door slamming mutely after lax linen-slack behind. In minuscule letters in the minuscule moleskin, MacBeth's noting: *What then is the pleasure of a discourse? In which one no longer means*: Courage, Camille?

He waits.

He waits [mouse scurrying in wall].

The Second Surveillant

4:50p. And day's final filtered trace abruptly snuffed by street lights. So railway-flat Room, indelible in middle, emitting air of stagnant or impregnable into night beyond casement. Where, with vigour, as in an operetta, myriad successive illuminations, fused by cheap electric current from giant Northern rivers, rendering our town the bright-est lit on continent. Maximum highrise office windows. Cheeky billboard neons. Multicoloured tree lights [notwithstanding season]. Spangles. Bangled circus rides + bridge spans. That fluorescent cross on mountain. Plus, to make the point completely: giant rotating beam atop cross-shaped edifice in middle of the city. Faintly caressing, in passim, tip of skylight on 4999 Settler-Nun roof.

—But did she ever return?

The deemed-dead-or-disappeared agoraphobe in window opposite. Glancing down at icy 4999 Settler-Nun court. Whence, ca. 4:50p, antique sheepskin gliding out. Then up at top-floor casement. Where, upon seeing no ~~exergue~~ *Face* [only geeeze flying over], the recluse fading into shadow. Reappearing — to incredulity of a passer — in own second gallery door. Lean pink-wool crewneck, grinning at lover the postman. Bounding up slippery outer iron stairs in brimmed postie hat, singing at top of his lungs: —*Fi-ive go-olden ri-ings, four calling birds, three Fr-ench hens, two tur-tle do-oves.*

But did she return? Here we making do with document of little value: a police report. —*What does it matter que de-çi de-là, une erreur, une omission minime?* joking young assistant Jean-François Jean, student of Techniques policières, Collège de Rosemont de Montréal. Soundlessly closing bottom stairway oeil-de-boeuf door. Hoping that ancient Parisian ~~peeper~~ instructor, eternally glued to keyhole, head nodding somnolently, remaining in là-là land awhile. —*Far from we loutish Montréal constabulary aspirants*, lisping the student, flicking dismissive wrist in air. *Far from these endless arpents de neige! From this incomestable French-Canadian food, delivered sans concern for the bien of the citizen!*

And Jean-François Jean loping in semi-dark out Settler-Nun gate.

Indeed: In old gendarme's head, it's Paris. 1924. *A summer's stroll on outskirts.* Along canal Saint-Martin. Opposite the legendary malodorous abattoirs of old la Villette.

His adored Jos. Dousse strolling along beside. Pale shirt, pressed pearl-grey trousers, spats. Never had he, C-N Dupuy, met a man more impeccable in his linen. That almost wild animal smell. Which, not having ever been pursued by th' terrible breath of a grizzly, the Parisian, imagining fresh as a flower. Because wild animals don't overeat + shit regularly.

Peacefully, they stroll. C-N in soft leather boots, fashionable à l'epoque, laced to the ankle. Jos., exceptionellement, in sleeveless skin gilet, discreetly beaded + fringed at the neck. Causing certain heads to turn. The young gendarme's own further turning, perhaps, from stench of the abattoirs, the blood darkening earth, cement, water. Prompting one of those moments called boomerang in psychology. When ancient Casse-Noisette, on knees at Settler-Nun keyhole, geriatrically adrift in long bygone afternoon, walking by canal foul to point of overwhelming, retrospectively perceiving chink in Jos.'s heretofore perfect armour. A rather coarse flank Jos. that day, in striding beside with grace of a panther [thinking old cop lasciviously] choosing to reveal. Jos., pausing, about to tell a story, uttering: *NOW!*

—*Now. On that pahr-ticular afternoon I was apprentice to a boardwalk jeweller. Back in Pincher Creek, AB. Who would, comin' in from lunch, raise a cheek in cloudy trouser right off his seat. And let go a really tremendous smelly. So one day after lunch at th' China Man's, I/Jos. bringin' in a stink bomb. Fouler than foul, just as boss Joe Daly's settin' in his chair. Leanin' to th' left, right cheek raised a smidgen, about to let fly his afternoon toot — my stink bomb secretly released. Under workshop bench. Hideous. Ouash. Choke. Entire shop runs out.*

Meanwhile, young stagiaire's loping round block on crazy cramped legs. East on Mont-Royàl. North, Saint-Urbane. West, New-City. Back onto Settler-Nun again. Ten x round loop, passing florist picking syringes in entrance to alley. Plateau diaper dispensary. Neoned crack-house [open]. Closed Arab café. Second-hand camera vendor [empty of clients]. Yellow door of yellow-haired woman. Sleeping with fuzzy yellow dog, one yellow head increasingly resembling t'other. The stagiaire, a Catholic, i.e., knowing implicitly confession leads to redemption, but rarely to change in comportment. Valiantly resisting bifurcating South. Direction, l'École nationale de théâtre. Zone cased earlier, preparatory to auditioning ce soir for role of Ligéia [night-school production]. Having, on that [regulation] break, swung right, boul Saint. Wondering, trotting South, should he wear a dress? Or edgier without? Till, inevitably, on arriving in theatre's sketchy North-of-

Chinatown quarter, digressing into Montréal Pool Room + Steamies protracted double-room diner. Back-lit from alley, throwing in relief tired ads hand-painted boasting famous slaw-smothered chiens-chauds. Old boats of once-amazing fries. Faded clippings of great Hab♥ Maurice Richard. Map of quarter, 1927. Long nondescript counter, crunched foil salvers pretending not to be ashtrays. In back end of room, grey accountant-with-accoutrements [shiny blue shirt]. Adding numbers at the pool table. But now, ca. 5p, our stagiaire dutifully doing lap #10, down Settler-Nun, one block East. Two blocks North. One West, ere climbing, once more, 4999 outside iron stairs. Softly shutting brown-painted plywood oeil-de-boeuf door. Resettling pudgy derrière on black paint-chipped inner middle step, instantly registering that the steamy hotdog special [coke, deux chiens-chauds, triple frites] from official break two hours earlier. Totally digested. To point of hungry again. Sore-assed + bored, J-F giving yet

---

♥ Is not the historian's responsibility to ponder, above all, connections between name + object as mediated through communities of speakers? Thus, the moniker 'Habs,' as Montréal Anglos dubbing legendary local hockey team, a compression of 'habitant' [peasant], may be viewed as containing the ghost of an affect. Conversely, in French 'le Canadien' is the name of the beloved team — though the Franco population generally loath to personally identify as other than Québécois.

one more moment to hating that tapette uniform-fetishist, his progenitor. For sending him to police school. Ere bending profile, elegant as Ligéia's. Reminicent of ancient medallions of the Hebrews. And keying in rubrique: *Surveillance Report Assignment.*

Itching to add: *Subtitle, Dreamland.* Given his favourite method of gleaning, in semi-somnolent state, random hits from relevant surveillance intelligence. Having read in that junkie US queer, William Burroughs: all crime's a tampering with presumables. Therefore, deducing the youth: essentially in eye of the beholder [so much for what they saying at police school]. Potentially, behind Room door, was then both victim + suspect. A soul maybe teeming with anguish, being perpetually discomfited, like any one by intimacies of Others living stacked up vertically all around narrow court in middle. A set not architecturally unlike that of the overplotted [his opinion] Hitchcock noir *Rear Window.* Where in gaze of the narrator, line blurring admirably between murdered + murderer. Is the assassin ever entirely without her reasons? Possibly explaining why only one [ex] acquaintance of Settler-Nun person of interest noticing that risus sardonicus in 4999 railway-flat window no real Face. But frost scored on pane. And reporting R. Dousse missing. As per the message J-F Jean scoping on minuscule palm monitor:

Police officers from District 20 of le Service de police de la Ville de Montréal seeking individual living in Mile-End borough. Object of various complaints from neighbours; of late, reported as possibly missing. Though others claiming to see her face in upper 4999 Settler-Nun window several times daily. No bank nor credit card transactions for a week . . . .

And in one of those heady moments of youth-not-yet-overly-trying-to-please with ever more homogenizing locutions, the young stagiare's deciding to deploy, for final police assignment, regardless of consequences, the hazardous selection method inspired by André Breton's great novel *Najda*. Breton, who like himself, believing in labyrinthine structure of individual. Hence in incipient integration of life + art. Entailing, for purpose of assignment, arbitrary interception of target posts. Chat logs. Police cams in trees. Phone tabs. *Whatever*. Gleanings he ideally formatting into little rotating loops, disappearing/ appearing in no fixed order. Creating nifty multi-flash effect. Hélas that retard Parisian peeper — smelling increasingly like a funeral — wanting ten dactylographed pages. Oké, d'abord ... Bedroom eyelids dropping, head half-leaning back, J-F's scripting little random pickings into The Last Concession Ever.

SURVEILLANCE REPORT ASSIGNMENT
J-F Jean #59847193

Frame I: MySpace [audio file]:
        'Avatar of Public Transport, #80'
        2003-10-03

My friend, pure laine [but eyebrows of Huron], reading
from a book, quothes grandly: —*The urbanity imagined
here's still not anchored in the world imagination.* Passing
by the ridge called The Mountain — a few yellow re-
els hanging from branches — I forgive her. Has not she
made many under-takings on my behalf? Included me in
things? Still, I/R declaring loudly: — *The tragedy of this
place, so carefully chosen because it has all the veins running
through it running through myself. Is that I must leave. Do
you remember when the voyageurs set out from Lachine? Wool
socks, blessed crosses, ammunition?*

Frame 2: Microsoft Word Doc:
        e-journal_2002_06_01

Dear Diar-~~rhea~~: On refusing to tell birthdate for apartment
lease renewal, that bitch the landlord squawking — *Proof
you can't be trusted.* Luckily our mutual — unbeknownst
to her — shrink MacBeth, who, being human [he
pretending], incapable of 100 percent neutrality, identifies

with Bottoms. Like me. Albeit insisting on a base level Rosie can be sneaky. Being often, in head, anywhere but here. The worry gene, he calling it. Yesterday, he tediously invoking the cliché of childhood: a blank cheque, aged five. Plunked with clothespin on tongue at kitchen table. Having torn the plastic gingham tablecloth up in strips. From every pink-sheared notch. Then lying it was brother Jos., the ripper. Or was it my mouth washed out by Veeera's bar of ivory, he, Mac-Bee resuscitating? Leading to usual question: And what was she, that instant messenger Mama, cleaning? To steer him off, I said I dreaming that I/Rosine, in window, double of Grandpa's ex-fiançée, Dar-Dar Beaulieu. Former resident of Fanny Bendixon's Saloon in the historic town of Ed. Which fiançée, Grandpa saying, in a letter [after I/R announcing planning not to marry], he finding *one day, on returnin' home from huntin'. Walkin' the boardwalk. 'Now. Dar Dar,' I said, 'I can't marry you.' There were tears in her eyes.* MacBeth said nothing. Only remarking R cadence, in speaking, sometimes 'country,' sometimes 'Oxonian.' And why so much energy trying to fit in? Alternately withdrawing exhausted. Which deportment people finding confusing. I said: —*You're borrowing their excuses.*

Frame 3: Surveillance Cam [Content Analysis]

Vicinity, Café Nous:

2003-11-01, 15:00

Woman [credible resemblance to suspect] crosses Dada-Jesus. Enters Café Nous, corner Settler-Nun/rue des Magasins-Dispendieux. Frizzy pea duffel. Straddles red faux-leather stool at bright copper counter. Orders long espresso. Ludicrously discountenanced when coffee coming in minuscule little cup. Half the size of the cups they had before. Through the window, a student of the theatre, following the gestures, easily guesses dialogue:

—*Hey, what's with th' cups?*

—*My brother likes 'em* [owner grinning, embarrassed, hair wings flying over ears].

—*Tell your brother to go to hell!*

Frame 4: E-mail, Boîte d'envoi

De: r.negative

Date: 2003-10-01

A : xlander@pcan.ca

Objet: re:

My darling X: Today they asked me to trim your ROSIE [a thorn in the ambience]! It was war to the finish. On radio soldiers arriving boxed from Kandahar. Do you remember The Flame in S-D? Those army/navy girls shipping out to 'Eye-rack.' To this day, I/R smelling their elixir of desert eucalyptus. Sweet magnolia. Fragrant pepper. Outside, palms reaching down avenue past that bar named Cheetah. And up up into a night named Indigo. Keening like those char-rettes driven by the mysterious Métis [Grandma Prisc, *people claimin'*, grudgin' Dill on her deathbed]. The cousins, fat, skinny, tan or baked apple. Drinking Tia Maria in motel room near Pincher Creek, AB. Yelling they'd tell Peeet I calling him a half-breed: —*Gram-pa th' Indian. Your eyes, Rosine!*

X, sorree for raising that again.

Re S-D: do you remember scaring defrocked monkess in bedroom two floors up? By sitting straight up in bed, 3a, + screaming: —*Fuck you fuck you.* Cause disliking a certain three-ways pillow conversation: MOI: —*I'm creamin' in my pants!* TOI: —*A wet bird never flies at night!* SPEC-SARGE NAN: —*Then honey it just ain't wet enough.* Ha —she was special all right! For a sec, liking her more than you.

There could have been a murder.

Frame 5: Chat: 'r.negative'
       À: bottoms_bitch.com
       2003-09-17, 2:00
R-eeef, my Dad, in a dream
E-ating with my friends in boul Saint bar, flirtatious as
    usual

E-quals all the girls joking about deferral + Derrida. Reeef has to leave. For 'meeting with senior advisor to local Conservative.' Who

E-xpressing displeasure that girls like his daughter are not in what they call the reality-based community. Reeef replying that being a soldier himself, he knowing plenty of enlightenment principles + empiricisms. The guy cutting him off: That's not the way the world really works anymore. We're in charge now, + we decide what reality is. And while guys like you are studying that reality, we ll be creating other new realities, which you can study too. In the whole dream, the smell of intimate

F-lesh or chicken soup.

Frame 6: Boîte de réception:

De: Boubou Delaney

Date: 2003-09-01

Objet: Adieu

Bonjour, Rosine. Frankly, it surprises Agathe + me you want to meet. After attacking us like that in Cinéma du Parc. Clearly, your mental state's precarious. We regret you are bitter. You know we included you in things, dinners, cultural events, drives to the country. The other night, waiting in line for popcorn [best, says Agathe, in the city], we saw that scary look in your eyes riding down the escalator and said in unison: *Attention! Here she comes!* Pupils dilated like that day we were walking on Hotel-of-the-City. And I made the mistake of jesting you're *une bonne anglaise dans la mesure du possible.* Your fists were clenched like that, last night, walking toward us. Every friendly word betrayed by incompatible tics + gestures. Finally, you aggressed Agathe when she said, to be *sympa*, that you feel invisible here because coming from the West. Riposting right up in her face — *And you're a typical xenophobic franco!* We, here, are known for our tolerance. But your physiognomy, crossing the Marienbad Square floor, plus the black pantsuit [I find them unattractive on women], necktie, etc., left, I assure you, a strong impression. Adieu.

Frame 7: Personal Surveillance Video
      [J-F Jean]
      Parc Settler-Nun, 2003-10-06
I [Cadet Jean] sitting on a bench [camera in sleeve]. Leaves falling around fenced-in tennis courts. Dealer pitbull closing in behind. Woman on bench beside. Jean-jacket leaning forward. Strong resemblance to Jeanne-Mance target of surveillance. Eyeing, like a stalker, towering brunette, white tennis dress. Whose nervous leg, in serving, goes up too dramatically, causing loss

of balance. Pitbull moving in. As if knowing what I'm up to. Dealer in shadow of maple pretending not to notice, studying silver light of clouds. At end of bench, guy with accent [possibly a client]. Likewise leering [or pretending], at legs of tennis beauty. Suddenly he shouts to stout companion on bench beside:

—That guy's a Stalinist! He can fucking destroy you--

—Eat shit, man!

—I'm tryin' to raise your consciousness, + I'm th' one that's hateful?

Frame 8: Microsoft Word Doc:

'My e-Journal' 2003-10-21

Today, Dear Diary: I am offering a parable, despair, love + public transport having brought us to this. 'I/Dark Eyes' [X, you used to love them so much!] riding on #80 South. Caustic tic-tic in stomach risking little brown puddles, due to unfortunate incorporation of inimical reprimand from. I forget. Notwithstanding undeniable stellar self-presentation. Leather jacket tapering at waist, padded shoulders, black cigarette jeans, wave falling over ~~crow's eye~~ intense gaze. Emblematic of individuals loving only good for the Human Race. Therefore refusing to reproduce. Unlike my ancestor, Great-Grandpa Dousse, primogeniture of countless. Who, as a youth, before family paddling West, carousing with Shale Pit Workers! on Crystal Palace grounds. Singing: *Je t'plumerai la tête.* But never on a Sunday. When in ironed shirts, diligently soaped + scrubbed. Marching after Mass in proud procession to l'Évêché de Montréal. Behind wagons high with perfect hued stone for building Basilica. At cortège's head, firemen on horses. Crowds gathering, applauding these pious men. Daily doing extremely hard labour. Their shiny healthy faces, a vibrant response to all those insults directed against the unique French-Canadians. Destined by History to endless struggle for survival. Bus swerving South, toward centre of city. Chauffeur crooning falsetto: I/R, on back corner seat, taking in, to jingling of outside leaves + panting blue sky, Greek, rolling French, then, a little down aisle: soft-hard English. —*People don't know what it's like to be Indian!* And locating blue-eyed lady on right-side bench. —*People can say what they want. If they have body hair, they're NOT!* I/R wanting to get up. For purpose of descending aisle + thrusting hairless arm under nose of woman now yelling: —*People don't know what Indians have gone through.* Frilly-scarfed Greek friend beside, thoughtfully, distractedly:

—*My daughter's an Intimate Messenger.*

Frame 9: san_diego.pdf
Have you seen the Hokey Okee drag king? Little cheeks

wiggling in blue-jeaned ass. Baseball cap sideways over tight three-day jaw. Workboot bopping. To reconstructed hillbilly tune. In The Flame in town of S-D. Rosine sits watching. All the white to brown to black necks of enlisted navy chicks. In their flaming necklaces. She is slightly older. *Oh par-don! The whole family lied.* Skin significant carmel. Hair dyed mahogany. Outside a freeway of CITIZENS racing past palm trees. Pointing, nosing, like her grandpa's shiny shoe, in + out of gaps of opportunity. Smooth as sharks sliding ominously along a cobalt wash [in the Cousteau documentary]. From one lane to other, back, forth, any lane you want. Braking's badly seen. Unlike in Can-Can, where they have the passing lane for daredevils + regular for conformists. She heaves her small breast. Wanting to go to Paris. The shadows in the bar are like in a Hitchcock noir.

Frame 10: Boîte d'envoi

> De: r.negative
>
> Date: 2003-09-04
>
> À: MacBeth@Coddar.com

Dear MacBeth, as requested, for your voyeuristic purposes: my regressive morning pages. I/R having failed to replace what needing to forget with real-time absorption of external phenomenological experience: *Wed., 6a: Might I here describe the fragility of her smile? Arriving [the last time] in airport. Beret plunked bizarrely on head. Lavender scarf end dangling, like Isadora's. Jauntily to feet. Grey oval face turning aside on faux-marble floor. Meaning her stay not, hélas, reducible to the Act. She said she packed her gloves. But, irrevocably, in the absence of she with whom she in the Act of violating our unviolable luv [she spelt it like that], I/R growing tired from lying awaiting the accomplishment. Stiff beside. À propos, returning in taxi from Baroque Architecture Exhibition, conversation re: the countless models for dreamed-of Baroque mansions + official buildings. Elegant geometric stairs triangulating. Circling, pentagoning. Octagoning. Coning. Up chiaroscuro façades. Designed by best period architects. Then never even started! —S'oké, I/R remembering repeating. Trying to fall asleep untouched. Untasted. Beside. Do not sheep bleat in the word 'couple'? Thank God for winter. Weather-sealing people [Wo Es war, soll Ich werden]. True, at night sometimes, awaiting your taxi from the airport, getting up + walking down streets. Feet in autumn leaves. A shadow rustling behind.*

Possibly an ancestor.

A CLOU IN R CASE

On the bus to Kelowna, she suppresses a giggle. Nearly night. And the bus smells of bus. Her hair is straighter than usual. A guy, claiming to be Beothuk, hunted like animals till extinct, wants to take her picture. Wants her to dress up in traditional dress + pose. She has an interesting face. She thinks of herself doing town halls across the prairies reciting Pauline Johnson poems. The air is very dry. There has been a drought. Two years of forest fires + dust. Now in the middle of the night, a few flakes of snow fall outside the window, hitting a billboard stuck among some field scrub. WE WILL NOT REGISTER OUR GUNS. She must ask Auntie Dill. Dawn + the bus brakes down a slope. Past pens of waking bellowing calves nosing sparse yellow tips of grass. The odd cougar, they say. Auntie Dill will be waiting. Sitting straight + already dressed for hours. In the pink sweater with the seed pearls sewn on it. A great deal of costume jewellery made of real gold. Slingback heels. Her eyes, lashes curled with a lick of mascara, still clear as a bell. The determination that made her get out of bed with a slipped disk after falling off a horse. Because they were going on a picnic + Grandpa said if she couldn't get out of bed she certainly couldn't come. 'We were having fried chicken. Treats like that we hardly ever got.' The injury has plagued her ever since, now she hardly walks. At night sleeping flat on her back, knees raised over huge square box. Later same afternoon, sitting in some coffee chain where she has wheeled Dill in her chair, Dill sticking out her slingbacked foot threateningly at cars, crossing the four-lane road. Diabetic, she's eating pecan cake. And recalling getting married. 'The invitations were ready. Then Grandpa came in + said he was goin' huntin'. There wouldn't be any weddin' then. We had to order new invitations.' . . . .

113

Notown [The East]

Here, it behooves I/~~Basement~~ Bottom Historian, to surface. *Encore.* For purpose of resetting intrigue on path to dénouement. Even if believing, with all lucid spirits, that to plot is to parody remembrance. There being no redemption in ~~origins~~ extinct matter. Remembrance concerns not the dead. But what is alive + speaking within us. Do not skyscrapers bear, deep within, straw huts? The person, her ancestors? Hair. Cunt. Sweat. Going out, trying to look friendly. In case of someone [likely dead Veeera]. In back of head whispering: — *Don't stick 'em out like that, I know what you're up to.* So that R Protagonist ever after: slumping a little. Simultaneously ultra-admiring the insouciant perfect posture of French girls. Not to mention blonde future princess's in *Dial M for Murder.* White neck stem-up from red lace cocktail-dress caplet. Revealing perfect smooth collarbone skin. Tiny diamond pendant. Delicately pointing down to breasts small + pert. About to go guilelessly to prison. For stabbing the second-hand car salesman:

No guilt here.

Inversely, R Protagonist all twisted on bed. In dream of long-dead Veeera. Wasted, accusing, on a plane: —*My daughter. Is lying. About her origins. Which is why. Her personal relations. Trumped + false. As per usual.* Then, as any plane, distancing into yonder blue. And body on bed relaxing into elegant port de tête of little toddler Rosie. Who delighting everyone with her posture. Ere flexing neck forward again, on account of recent flush by Boubou + Agathe. Likely for failing to establish relevant coded contact, in what unsaying around them.

Reader, you may be forgiven for asking: what, here, is a ~~novel~~ life? If endlessly eclipsing into the emptiness of the middle? May we offer a clou in R case. A solid griffe or claw from 'the past.' Which time-worn device [analepsis]. Deployed in wider *Noir* genre. By way of photo inset. Or scintilla. The past + its objects, as saying great Walter B. Solely graspable in present as fragment or flash of illumination at moment of extreme contradiction. Implying any flickering planetary molecule [+ its shadow, memory]. Animate or inanimate. Capable of unexpectedly impacting any other. Which, when understood, fully. Will restore to rightful status the discerning Indigenous peoples. Who knowing nothing happening in any one planetary domain or moment. Ever definitively lost to any other.

*

THE PAST: Confronted with the racket of Catholics opposite. Veeera felt like smashing someone's face. Her beige lip also twitched when the Notown Fair gypsies spoke to her in French. The other element of her struggle: Reeef. R aforementioned Scots progenitor. Who in the middle of a Pincher Creek, AB, family porch argument one summer dusk, 1963. Re: what Catholics eat when eating the body of Christ. Eyeballing the empty August horizon, shimmering out a-d i-n-f-i-n-i-t-u-m. And muttering:

—*Movin' back East!*

—*Montréal?* Grandpa, the-tap-dancer-cum-jeweller's bird eyes fizzling in hard prairie light. Cupid bow smirk, remembering that priest, ca. 1924, Mile-End, QC. Soutane in slush. Gesticulating up at madame Maude David [not her real name]'s dark-brick second-storey cop brothel. Corner Clerks-Viateur + boul Saint. The madame in turn gazing down at priest's bulging orbs of a seiche + murmuring: —*Do you not know, mon Père? I, also, am a miracle of the stars. Plus, I am informed of your bad deeds against me. Sois conscient, je vous défends de venir frapper avec empressement. Trois fois de suite. Est-ce qu'on ne pense pas qu'une personne peut être couchée?* Priest's wiggly fingers oscillating South. Toward second house, re-*puted* [now La Cucina]. Not to mention yet another on diagonal from

Father's own orotund-domed Church. Whose unique mid-façade boy Jesus gazing sublimely o'er police ringing bell of establishment. Where girls + games of belote — *Parbleu! We know the power of that!* —disappearing during raids. Right through secret panel to triplex adjacent: —*Love thy neighbour, Father,* Maude David finishing. From smoky-lemony-spicy-magenta-curtained window. A piano played backwards. —*In Montréal, Beelzebub reigning,* pronouncing Grandpa. Glancing at his skinny #2 girl Veeera. Not his favourite. The second chapter never works. You can see that in novels.

Still, she got Reeef, a Presbyterian. Montréal-born. But predestined [by Grandpa] to stop at Québec province border. Sundays, fiddling on verandah 'Hot Garters,' 'St. Louis Square Stomp' + 'Turkey in the Straw.' Eyeing his little brat Rosie — a real bébé là-là in pink dresses, hand-piquéed by Veeera, missing her Catholic mother Prisc back in Pincher Creek. Rosie, who launching off steps under gaze of village women. Behind their curtains. Skipping up + down hill. Good legs in fold-down socks, patent shoes, direction: Notown Cemetery. Past the drunken barber's. Past store with sticky flypaper in window. In whose backroom the pale choc'late man flucking that horse-lady Lolita. Haich's Hard. Where Javex/Jav-elle. Under pale skies, thunderheads deeply puffing on pine-sweaty earth, on square brick houses the settlers building with their nostalgie. Saying Grandpa, so forest encroaching to the banks of the mighty cold Saint L. Crawling with industrious Glengarrians. Meaning soon nearly no forest nor Indians left. Save those marrying the [crazy] French. Does not true justice transpire where there are *just* Presbyterians? So they *thinking*, scoffing Veeera. Opening, in cedar-lined Notown attic, a cedar-lined trunk: some lady's burgundy velvet suit, strapped shoes. For taking the train ride to the great French metropolis.

The Man From Glengarry went in the stove: Veeera knew the score. People sans possibility of origins, losing links. In the wake of Others. Was not 'Grandpa,' as she calling her father, known back in Pincher Creek for hawking diamonds + reading tea leaves, saying certain individuals [~~her beloved dying mother~~ his wife] bearing the Seal of the ancestors?♥ He saw it in a teacup. Where, one day long ago also seeing his favourite granddaughter, Rosie. Black eyes, blonde curls, skating on future ice of

♥ No human lineage is certain. The family, like so many, fading on purpose quietly into background. Only answering when questioned: we know nothing beyond X generation. Not Grandma Prisc's proper family name. Nor the language Grandpa speaking when talking to his mother. Everyone knew the words of the new concept anthem: The Maple Leaf Forever.

big dark city. Something happening but winter keeps her warm. Entirely my sentiments, old man thinking. When beholding, in bottom of cup, time going on back. Out Room door. Stairs. Yellow leaves, also exiting court. What alarming Grandpa most: his little Rosie casting no shadow.

[Here, dear Reader, born of an instant's delight. Mere figment of the parents. Themselves pale projection of those going before. Here, we arriving in space where the sharp sensation something incontournable requiring our attention. For *IF* slushy footprints exiting court those same prints in Grandpa's leaky teacup. Then why, on this day of our lord, November 6, 2003, no silhouette, having earlier left court, now gliding back again up iron stairs, ca 5p? Used copy under arm of some good novel for reading during ice-storm. Say, *Kiss of the Fur Queen*. Plucked from pyramid of lezzy pulp, musky recettes, tired volumes of Deleuze, Derrida, Lévinas, at H's Recycled Books. Down boul Saint. Where H's man wrapping + telling, ultra-rapid (his wont), tales from old Europe. —*ElevenkidsinPoland. ThePolesforjokepullingolduncles beard. Tillbleeding. Onlythreesurviving. Sentoverhere.* Rosine, stroking flat-faced cat on counter, asking for bigger discount. —*It's in my nature*, she laughing. Retreating from H's man's

hurt physiognomy expressing *butalreadysoreduced!* Out
past two speed queens rushing in to sell books copped
from Dan's Used up street. Past Oscar animated-film
nominee panhandling on sidewalk. Small form ~~liking to
take a drink~~ bent geometric. Sun. Snow. Rain. Calling *Du
Change/Spare Change.* Infallibly matching language to
face. —*Spare change,* he saying to Rosie, in English. That
was an insult. She often complained, swinging on Settler-
Nun gate, back when neighbours copasetic, blending into
this so-called metropolis was like in childhood village of
Notown, ON: people going round deciding who to fre-
do-lin + who to blame.]

*

Disembarking at Notown Station [the East]: stock tongue
'n' groove walls, pot-bellied stove. And spring in the air.
Lilacs. Crabapples. Reeef, smiling rakishly, alongside
~~Veeera~~ his precocious little beauty Rosie. Already showing
more leadership in her little finger than most. Given her
way of walking. And soon. Playing tennis, swimming,
singing with will so strong. Does not the best come from
the West? Their skin not very dark, save in summer. When,
on arriving home from school, one breezy day. And opening
bevelled door off white-columned Notown house gallery.

121

Solid brick structure abandoned by owner of bankrupt cheese factory. Hearing Dill's raucous prairie laughter. Dill, in Veeera's pale, draped interior, who, on spying her little Rosie, jumping up off T-patterned sofa + screaming: — *THE CAT'S MEOW!* Hélas, Dill departing, leaving Veeera — eye fixed at edge of sunset [the West], iterating, almost driving Reeef crazy, that plants also shrieking when uprooted. Growing feverish. Leaving pot boiling furiously on stove. Inviting local hobos for Christmas, where discussing Old Testament verses before single bite of turkey. *And the Lord spake unto Moses. Saying speak unto the Children of Israel + say unto them. When either man or woman shall make a special vow to separate himself unto the Lord: he shall separate himself from wine + strong drink; he shall drink no vinegar of wine, or vinegar of strong drink, neither shall he drink any liquor of grapes, nor eat fresh grapes or dried. All the days of his separation shall he eat nothing that is made of the grapevine from the kernels even unto the husk.* Till Reeef 'movin' 'em' back West: Now, Haeckville, AB. Main street with false-fronted buildings. Climbed daily in small steps + gestes. Pulling in stomach. Jeans baggy from losing weight. Behind brother Jos. Looking mean but isn't [tight jaw, couple days' growth]. Smiling proud at attractiveness of his sister. Only hint of cruelty in air: rifle stashed behind driver seat of pickup. Parked on diagonal.

In front of Grandpa's Dousse Jewellers window: huge daffodil plunged between open pages of Bible. Sun slanting over grain elevators opposite. Inside, Uncle Peeet stalking pink pudding in polyester. As if a pheasant. Timelessness of mountains behind. The gay gap of prairie, flowered as a boudoir. You don't get used to no events. She wanted to go to Paris. *Christian College*, replying Grandpa. *At San Diego.*

Dial M[ontréal] for Murder

Thus, R Protagonist one day, late premillennial, stepping off Greyhound, rue René-Lévesque, Montréal, Québec. Walking North from bus station. Wearing hope + new charcoal winter coat. Mustard collar. Matching tam. Purchased in semi-tropical San Diego. Some people always leave. In her case, a day, when, exceptionally:

It was snowing on the freeway. And S-Diegans, unbelieving that the vicissitudes of nature should interrupt their rapid sked-duels. Pointing, nosing, sliding. Ungraciously into others. While Protagonist on child's bed Grandpa's friend, the defrocked monk's wife had given her. Masturbating loudly. Monk wife slamming bedroom door. R star boarder slamming open again. Walking out under underpass. Through sketchy [monkess's words] crystal-

123

meth quarter. Street curving curving down. Till fingering beautiful glittering port way below. The bright stars above. Plus satellite. Blinking mid lights of planes. Endlessly plunging toward harbour. High palms, sighing almost biblically against blue indigo. Crowded on the darkness of corners: fleecy-hooded illegals. Slipping into bus shelter. Scoping, in back of eye, wrecked queens in bobbed wigs. Lamé shades. Old white sailors in open shirts. Jeans. Three days' growth. Manfully restrained stomachs. Milling about en-trance of bar named Cheetah. Staring hostilely. Meaning R Protagonist abruptly turning. Up slope again. Past fan palms, hibiscus, medicinal eucalyptus. *Bail Bonds* screaming from backs of bus-stop benches. Having, by circuitous route of *substitutive satisfaction*, left monkess's casa door open. Risking her getting murdered. By some bozey parker from zoo lip opposite. Always already knowing monkess's fat finger's dialling cops to clear out bozey parker bag nests. Scoped through upper ~~echelon~~ storey window. Hélas, I/R lacking legal package. Every citizen having.

Speaking of analepsis: on said late premillennial day, Rosine Dousse, getting off bus in our wintry Metropolis + walking North in her little coat. Seeing soft snow also

falling in little glass boules. In older shop windows up +
down boul Saint. Each little glass boule with snow falling
in it showing a different festive drinking incident. Precisely
all the same glass boules in all the same shop windows as
on this current first snowy day, November 6, 2003. Save
snow now instantly eclipsing into freezing rain. To snow.
To rain. Back to driving snow again. Pushing people
North. Here,

Reader, in interest of dénouement, let us follow
silhouette dégageant from wind-battered crowd. Thin +
bright as high winter air. Air ringing with echoes of those
going there before. Inc., her own little inner premillennial
Rosie, fresh off the bus working. Soon very very hard.
—*Yet never getting what I want*, she complaining that
day swinging on Settler-Nun gate. Had not she, Rosine
Dousse, been fooled again? In coming to this place? —*Just
like young Saint Paul, in th' Bible. Accusing old Saint Jerôme
of somehow misleading. To which th' older man replying that
he, Jerome, would not, but he, the younger Paul, could still
achieve greatness.*

Now R silhouette striding toward parc. Ice pellets
pummelling head, face, ears. Coating thin-clad shoulders
of homeless woman, sobbing just ahead: —*Mother! Don't
feel/or obligatory need to part/for sake of your daughter/with
money won at bingo!* And laminating sidewalks. Courts.

Iron stairs. Façades. Fenestration. Middle gallery entrance. Rat-tat-a-tatting mingling with murmuring distant rush of branches, in uneven lash of storm. While

Behind Room door:

Telephone ringing. Ah

That instrument of love. Causing inner-stairwell assistant to raise head a minute. Jostling keyboard in nodding off again, therefore failing to perceive new rush of pixels converging on monitor.

You could smell th' venison cookin'. In th' kitchen. Frenchy tobacco Grandpa rollin' into cigarette. Not to mention th' smell 'a Veeera's crack. In those days laden with evil portent. On sofa bed. Where restin' her shapely hips. Th' little bulge in stomach hearin' future mama(n) thinkin': Stuck already. Four months + bored. Bored. BORED. --*What to do for th' rest of my tether?* On cue, Reee-ferent enterin'. Smell of snow on green wool of uniform. Dried lips from chain-smoked cigarettes. The family reeked of sex. Dill's eye under mascara, bright as a birdie's, watchin' Grandpa's lips, thin to point of cruel. About to tell a story. Somebody fartin'. Cousin. Brother. Uncle. You can smell their eagerness beneath their shirts. The girls still waitin' to be married. Gettin' release by squeezin' maze of pimples on each other's backs, upstairs in Grandma's bedroom . . . .

The assistant nodding on. Bedroom eyes awash with whirling electrons. Invading all his channels. Full mouth, chin, gently bobbing, hinting at future embonpoint of one liking his beer. Revelling — just as sandman gluing curly lashes definitively asleep — in impression that, unlike their arthritic-brained elders, who're perpetually getting off on dirty secrets, post-millennial sleuths, more to the point, are wondering why dirty secrets, given everybody having, still being paraded as mysterious. Waiting for his queue at Montréal Pool Room + Steamies, J-F Jean has often been known to reflect on how totally beyond this *Histoire de l'oeil* his generation is. Being more canny. Like Ligéia, whom no maid ever equalling. The radiance of an opium dream. Determining, post-demise, to remain strategically distante. Knowing her lump of a husband, in prematurely remarrying, inevitably soon hating the insignificant Rowena. With a hate more demonic than human. The assistant, in his blissful half-somnolent state, absorbing entire sounding moment: dog yelp. Decrescendo of homeless chick deeper in parc: —*Hey! No need to contact th' city's finest/if not getting from yours truly/th' intellectual uplift expected.* Poly-plink of rain to ice to rain on roof. Voice crooning, —*Baby, it's cold outside.* Himself, safe in dreamy silky space. Of Ligéia's former castle boudoir. Lined with folds of tapestry. On floor. And covering ottomans. And ebony bed. Scene infinitely more in shadow than set of *Dial M for Murder*. Where 'man of promise,' formerly at Cambridge, teeth white + shiny. Notwithstanding humble beginnings. Theatrically rehearsing with accoutrements, for coming murder. Gloves. Cane. Key under carpet. Sadly, given history has two classes, the amassees + the masses. The amassee — instead of herself either becoming dead on dining-room floor. Or on gallows for murder. Charming faux-gullible Scotland Yard constable, with help from her crime-writer lover, to try new narratives. Till ultimately proving hubby a loser not only in tennis. But also in game of ~~self-preservation~~ positive dénouement. Here we have a clou in R case. The shadow of a motive straying into Room. Where lying R Protagonist. Eyes wide open. A voice somewhere, opining:

 —Rosine is a liar.

They sang that tune in Notown. Its handful of citizens strung out in houses along a street called Broadway. So shiny + icy in winter, moonlit children skating after ice storms in direction of the uncontrollable contigency, the ice-heaving Castor [i.e., Beaver] River. Over whose gently curving bridge the little pink ruched dress running. First past troubled Main Street businesses. Empty as caskets [snorting Veeera]. Their dried fly-spotted contents no longer mirrored as essential, mocking Reeef. Who, exceptionally in that town: having a job. Running, running — his little Rosie's blonde curls are blowing. Ignoring leak of light [there's always a crack] behind village curtains. Running along sunlit side of pines like those outside Grandpa's, back in Pincher Creek, AB. Jays, screaming in boughs, Grandpa chasing on behalf of his robins. Calling them, respectively, Protestants + Catholics. In all towns: yet another graveyard for Anglicans. But the tomb cannot really leak into light of day, thinking Rosie. Climbing Notown Anglican cemetery stone wall + jumping. Arms flapping, hitting ground hard. Climbing up + jumping again. Arms flapping harder. Hitting ground. Climbs. Flaps. Hits. Climbs. Flaps. Hits. Head. On piece of extruding encrusted stone. Now going batter. Better. Jumps. Flaps. Feels landing less. Lying on ground, floaty clouds overhead running amok: —*I know how to fly*, Rosie yelling. Skipping up + down back over curved iron bridge, heaved block ice glittering white under. Past bright-roofed houses of women, breasts + pointed napes. Thinking that kid, on account of Daddy being in the Forces, going somewhere [not to court]. Racing, little sweat beading upper lip. Past Cousie's Garage. Coke ads + girly calendars. —*Why you not home helping yours?* shouting from raised garage door, son of that mother who only true Indian left. But Rosie, running, yelling wildly to huge DoDo Marotte, telephone operator, herself, heading toward bridge. From opposite direction. —*I know how to fly!* Th' kid's a liar, thinking DoDo, huge form turning + watching little staggering back.

Like th' rest.

Two Blocks Over, MacBeth

[Heart so white]. Framed once more in steel geometry of proto-deco window directly over Collège Socrate pennants: *Français. Grecque. Japonais*, etc. Scoping dark-skinned French-immersion lovelies. Exiting the building. His own skin, save spots high on the cheeks from papa's Celtic predilection for booze, likewise very smooth. Resembling, in profile, the classy dead object of graffiti under side-alley window: *Trudeau Rapace!*♥ Looking down again. The busty girls're hustling out college door. Big earrings. Lacy embroidered mules. In style this year. Linge tres blanche. Knowing how to fold a shirt, *you bet!* He, Étienne MacBeth, is shocked he thinking that. Really. Wanting nothing from 'them.'

A dozen tiny planes, buffeted by wind, grasshop up above, one, then another, through spot of blue into fluffy piling white. A laundry ad, you could say.

♥To call dead Prime Minister Pierre Elliott Trudeau "rapace" [bird of prey] borders on confusing to those Anglos who considered him a shining, emblematic hero. But for many Francos, his declaring Canada not bi- but multicultural cast a shadow, rendering French-language culture non-exclusive in the Canadian federation, therefore in danger of being swallowed. Further, the acronym PET, in the day used mockingly in Québec, means fart in French.

Another client, late. He waits. Hand placed on stomach. Full of the empties. The tweedy knees of his trousers bending, the better to scope large 'coolie' [word repressed immediately] hatted Asian. Leaning o'er green bottle-recycling bin. Below. Is not this acerbity in stomach less attributable to coffee [excellent Armenian torrefacteur's Ethiopian Yirgecheffe espresso]? Than to letter from that arrogant Willman's lawyer across apartment back court. Charging him, MacBeth, with harrassment, following the sleepless psychoanalyst's carefully worded missive re: muffling the terrier. Face splotches empurpling again. What makes those bastards think they're so entitled? Like Israelis in Palestine. Then MacBeth recalling someone saying:

—*Willman a Dane.*

I'm a racist, he thinking. Somewhat disconsolately. Spreading endlessly washed fingers. Over dilating tummy. Missing Rosie. With her it's not work. Always bringing news, filling them from crown to toe with direst amusement. Their burning mouths over burnished desk. Hoarse from secrets + feuilletons. Last time, the ground-floor Potter from Oregon — M shrinks them all — heard by Rosie through backcourt window. —*Having sex for*

a change! Oomph... Oomph ... she mocking. —I waiting for
more. But already it over!

—Hardly seeming, MacBeth laughing [not to his credit],
worth the effort.

Gazing sideways, the tinny blue sky's turning hard silver-
grey. Behind racket of billboards. Behind fibre-glass
siding covering several formerly fantasical old cornices
+ pediments. Ordered, turn of 20th, from San Francisco
catalogues. No more fluffy clouds. Nor little grasshopper
planes. One helium balloon. Hanging low over wingspread
angel on that old carpetbagger-Father-of-Confederation
George Cartier's monument. Decked with angels,
British lions, crowning orbs. For a time shrouded, as if
to keep off tamtams, jugglers, homeless kids passing huge
superannuated syringes in full view of tourists.

—O why [sniggering MacBeth] *have they clad ye in the*
raiment of others?

On dark edge of parc, Thin Man high-stepping. Dehy-
drated. Eclipsing with little paper bag of syringes toward
bevelled-glass-façade washrooms at mountain's foot.
Blonde cleaner girl. Her red municipal truck surely

parked out front, this time of day. Holding mop + honking. Honking. To get the stoners out. MacBeth consults his watch.

L'horloge ne dort pas.

Thin Man back-channelling across perspective. Weird peripatetic dance contourning slatted garbage receptacle. Overflowing with horribly reeking plastic dog-shit baggies. Cop car ignoring. The featured crime this week: unleashed puppies. Riling up doggy crowd. One in awful French: —*What about syringes in the grass. It's our park, get the homeless out!* —*It's the city's,* franco cop retorting. Soccer Mom complementing picture. Screaming patients from Hotel-of-God Hospital, ivs in arms, copping hits, wheeling hospital paraphernalia behind.

MacBeth opens parabolic drawer: Rosie, unseen for a week. Unseen again today. *Halfway between melancholia + paranoia,* he writes in his minuscule book. *Not being authorized to mourn, leaning increasingly toward latter. She thinks she's being watched, when being watched, she —*

From drawer with floral locket, the therapist's selecting bowl-locked Miss Kitty pipe. Grass. Grass of the parc.

Instantaneously greener. Autumn leaves more orange. Flying off booted toes of sashaying girl. Good French bangs. Her tight little undies blowing somewhere on line. Dropping hand of T-shirted six-packed dude, she's forging into traffic of users. Blokes♥ with toe-out bedroom-slipper shuffle. One disguised as Mexican in sombrero. Panhandling by Banque Nationale. One in tunic collar, very dark eye circles, sliding, elegant, exhausted. Onto bench by low gas-station-yard brick wall. Junior women cops on corner. Blonde bobs or tails, very clean shirt backs, pointedly to scene. Sun glinting off solid pairs of waistbelt cuffs, Rosie's preferred accessory. —*Now*, she always saying, in starting a story. Then speaking so fast she brutally destroying syntax. Punctuation + the right adjectives meaning nothing. Breathlessly asserting her visual, auditory, olfactory impressions. The steam rush of emotion bursting every clamp of restraint. Her sole preoccupation being to impress him with every vibration of some sexual encounter. Say, that woman-in-uniform under High Bridge in Haeckville, AB. Who first placing revolver on dash. Then cuffing Rosie to wheel —

♥ Reader, in this town a person could talk about the vagaries of naming forever. 'Bloke' = old term used by Francophones to designate Anglos, implying someone a little square. And the classic Anglo term for a Franco? 'Pepsi'!

Below, heavy post-meridiem grid of shiny metal bubbles. Creeping noisily over macadam. Speaking of 'syntax' [hand still on stomach] — maybe still woozy from yesterday's incomparable afternoon with lover from Flatbush. Whose singing ass on very white sheets he worshipping immoderately. The therapist getting up from desk. And dancing little step to the dub music in head. Feeling [though pushing 50] pretty cool. —*Would you dance with me in public?* he asking lover. Who replying cautiously: —*That depending where*. Down in alley: still no client. Only fat kid pissing on *Trudeau-Rapace* graffiti. And enthusiastic woman shouting confidentially to neighbour:

   —*Tomorrow we are having*
      Chili-encrusted salmon.

MacBeth writes in tiny little book: *Dispersal: a mental state relating to paranoia. Inasmuch as emanating from resolute overfocus on current accident to be avoided.*

He lights his little Miss Kitty odour-proof paraphernalia. And takes a toke. Are not all paranoids self-fulfilling prophecies? He puts the bowl-locked odour-discreet Miss Kitty back in drawer.

MacBeth turns out the light.

'Veeera'

The Crypt's Tale

Were one kneeling 'omniscient' in back-shadow of geometric cornice. Peeking through turn-of-20th glass + iron skylight raised on 4999 Settler-Nun's tar-+-gravel roof. Down into railway-flat Room, enhanced occasionally by backlight from some roving highrise rooftop beam. Then she, on bed under, having air of repeatedly rearranging. Her *Face*, now dark, accusing, as old soul's Veeera. In next haphazard slant: cute fat cheeks of Grandpa's little fis'. Yet again, sweet bleached profile on bus from Christian College in town of S-D. Or the angry glare seen earlier in upper railway-flat window. O'er second-gallery oeil-de-boeuf door. Onto which door pasted eagle-claw poster. For Aboriginal literary festival. To impress all the liberals. Rest assured, dear Reader, far from parsing these scintillae in air, our novel, in nearing dénouement, shall still meander. Incommensurate as fashion. Where *after* ever citing modes of *before*. As in that 40s horizontal-knit striped dress round Rosine Dousse's ass, bending over police reporter desk. Or the tweed-patterned cap from her matante Maddie [Trotskyist] sycophant, smoking outside Groupe marxiste révolutionnaire HQ. Or, grey buttoned-to-bottomskirt, + jacket, for mourning, tearless, at Veeera's [premature] funeral. Or glasses that darken, groovy, under Cafe Nous fluorescents, while energetically maintaining to Agathe, Boubou, Notebook — or any individual pretending flatness of affect typiquement anglaise — that her old friend, Father B of Prince Albert, SK, always saying, in ministering to the mixed-ancestry people of his far-North parish: — *Th' hybrid rising above her dichotomies. With the clarity of autumn. Unless stuck in the crack. Of her belongings* —♥. So

Is she lying there next ~~th' absent one beside her~~ stuck like that? In th' gloaming? Plus several seconds you-can-hear-a-pin-drop. Ere broadcast voice belting down Settler-Nun hall. From yellow kitchen radio. Declaring, with certainty of top-paid state-radio employee just arriving from Europe. That clearly French identity thing no longer relevant. He saw that in Paris. Local accent retorting:

—*Here comes truck with independence leader's big face on it.*

—*Haw. Haw. Haw. Call in your small animals.*

♥ 'Michif-speaking people always like to joke. They always like to say things, you know, to get you going + to have fun. One of the main things that kept our health up was our laughter. So if I told you something, as a Métis person, and if you were a white person and I approached you and told you something that I thought would be funny … it would be insulting to you. So when you're looking at the whole picture of health and of culture, that's a very important point.' [John Boucher, 'Michif Language Background Paper' (National Aboriginal Organization on Health)]

Meanwhile in railway-flat stairway: old Casse-Noisette, éternellement on knees. Bony fingers thin-to-point-of-disappearing in greeny stairway air. Characteristically squeezing hanky to nose + holding loupe steady with chilling patience of sleuths, spies, police agents of so many decades' experience. You wouldn't believe it. Hairy ear catching contralto somewhere uttering: —*I wanted to fuck you all night.* Jolting old gendarme, inchoately, toward boul Saint, Montréal, QC. Ca. 1924. His youth, still unquaffed, hastening North toward Maude David's brothel. In search of only man he ever really loving. Passing countless tavern windows. Patrons reaching for glasses to accompaniment of music. Streetcars. Rag-trade women rushing along narrowing boul Saint ribbon. Disappearing into pinky-turquoise at end of horizon. Which horizon bouncing off panes on either side of street. Bouncing in turn off each other under fantastical oriental cornices. The Parisian skipping jauntily. Past old textile vendors. Shortening their rulers [which was probably advisable]. Past Little-Children-of-Jesus. Whose Latinate church shadow prayerfully extending toward then freshly erected sky-blue bathhouse opposite. In those days, strictly for ritual cleansing. Corner Fair-Mountain. Where stones flying in early dark. Hitting smoky tavern windows. Behind which Shale Pit Workers! swigging. [Children crying outside green tavern door: —*Papa, come home!*] Swigging swigging with dandruff-flaked peddlers from rues Colonial, Saint-Urbane, Griff-town. Flogging bare-assed ties to 'th' hicks.' And firefly yo-yos. Waterfall mugs glittering fluorescent. With falls quickening on tipping. Then repacked in sample cases + headed for River-of-th'-Wolf. Massawippi. Jolly Port. Cases stowed under seats of vendors. Parking white bottoms in cheap suits, boots, sole-lined with newspaper. In various conveyances heading North to th' boonies. Reading in *Le Journal*, *La Patrie* or *Herald*:

   Yesterday, savages known as Têtes-de-boules. Killing several wolves entre Matane et Rimou—

X, speaking of heartless purveyors, I just saw you floating over. Big tits in polka-dot shift, cinched in at waist heading down beach! But grant it, the purveyors were *before*. Before time was ripe. Before Ipperwash, Burnt Church, Port Radium, James Bay, Kanesatake, where handful of armed Mohawks stopping Caucasians from The Outers. Backed by th' army + provincial police. From destroying sacred burial ground for golf. Course. Oh X. Do you remember? On train to pow-wow under Two Mountains. All th' blue-uniformed conductors girls like us? [People were freer then.] Do you remember on approaching th' barricades: th' lawns in front of all th' ticky-tacky houses, pink flamingos

+ darky dwarves? Before people mostly learning not to say SAVAGE out loud. Albeit already knowing to say th' masses + amassees. E.g.: tenants + landlords. A latter of which. Contemporaneously Ringing. Ringing 4999 Settler-Nun middle gallery bell.

Quiet. Again. The electric current. That gift of the land inhabited by the soul of giant waterways formerly flowing North. Till cruelly torqued by men to flow in exactly opposite direction. Flooding caribou + poisoning every little poisson. With mercury. Generating, in process: current. Momentarily interrupted by ravages of ice storm. From flowing in cables o'er tundra. O'er o'er-exploited boreal forest. Till collapsing. With layer on layer of ice. So that now in Settler-Nun totally dark Room, the abruptly non-static ambience resonant with pummelling tamtamming of ice pellets hitting front blades of ploughs. Careening off the smaller sidewalk models also hurtling up rues Clarke. The Esplanade. Hotel-of-the-City. Coloniale. Henry-J. Drolet, Settler-Nun, etc. Pelting homeless chick. Crying, just ahead: —*What are you doing? I see your ill stupid doing. I see your dig ass of an ugly* ... Causing silhouette in dark end of Room to oscillate a little [*until we die there will be sounds!*]. On railway-flat bed. Possibly projecting, in lying there akimbo, unnice image. Simultaneously self-admonishing: La sécurité, c'est quoi? C'est ... suspicious, avaricious! Meanness. Of self-imposed seclusion. Who wanting to be 'secure'? No free spirit ever dreaming of 'security.' Or. If. She. Did. Laughing! Laughing! Letting others almost in range, then slamming middle gallery door. Causing postie, raising rain-brimmed hat, to be declaring, in handing mail through barely ajar crack, to lovely lips, with toothpick visible in corner.

   —*You're a bitter little lady.*

The Fly [Ex Voto]

Speakin' of *ressentiment*: If only this heart, commanded by love, not bindin' me to fretwork. Cheeks all red + puffy. Knowin', on cop stagiaire's purple monitor: Dill, erect at Grandpa's table. Plottin' to squash my once-upon-a-time greener-of-ichor person. As I th' baby musca skippin' analeptically onto plate rail. Where — flicked by Dill's tapette — I crawl across an angel. Climb a plaster pubis. Tired to point of reawakenin' a click. In glow of neige qui tombe. Th' dark November eve. Short'nin'. Short'nin'. And assayin' one more little stairway hocus-pocus. Simultaneously sensin' that tapette still in back of ample auntie hass on Grandma's share ...

That Dill will get me yet. I dos-i-dos behind th'
most expensive plate on Grandma's rail. No-she-no's
+ th' re-hearse. Stick my right foot out. And cop a
cookie crumb. Missed by Irish char. Who, asked by
Grandmama(n) to get down on her knees + wipe off
sixty spindle legs of faux Windsor chairs, squawkin' out
window to little Rosie, streakin' in frills + patent leather
shoes past th' row of pines with th' jays across th' street,
tryin' to take from Grandpa's robins: Your grandma's
a *squaw-k squawk squaawk*. Dill's fat fingers. Creepin'
behind her bratty prat again. Oh. Can you smell th'
roast on oval oak table? I/th' fly sidlin' slightly over. On
th' afternoon we are murdered, this story will become
malodorous. R little surrogate, at a loss without her
fly on th' wall, to secrete th' Méta Physique under th'
Topo Logic of reality. Of course she can come back
as a ghose. Oooooooh. Oh! Can you smell th juice? I
want to stick in my protuberance. Hélas only maintes
wars, revolutions, ecological disasters later when, due
to ephemeral materiality, certain sensory options
expired, will I get to DO IT: need I mention, th future
sé-lecte steak is Argentinean? . . . .

Here's where I cite Virgil: and the southern wind/
with a quiet creakin' of th' masts/calls us to

~~Eternity~~ Sleep — were not that coatless chick on
macadam whimperin, fainter. Fainter: —*I am a miracle
of the stars*. Then: fallin' to ground. In icy haze. Snow

blanketin' doucement over. Fallin' fallin' till she disappearin'. Completely invisible under. Just as snow blower turnin' right on Settler-Nun. Advancin'. Advancin'. Spewin' everything in front via high funnel over.♥ But we are loath to go ~~Father~~ farther. For we th' livin' obliged to keep movin'. Toward that monstrosity: th' future [+ th' anterior within it]. Though maybe failin' to make of destiny R time. Unlike that blonde in *Dial M for Murder*. Polished as a mirror. To catch R collective pathos. Yet, bred in th' bone, as Veeera likin' to say, for gold-plate survival. Magnificent in th' famous movie trailer. Her splayed manicured fingers gropin' gropin' for pointy scissors. On table behind. You get used to havin' no events. After havin' too many. So R future princess knowin' innately to look wan, hesitant. When temporarily languishin' in little stuffy cell or chamber.

Oh X, do you remember th' day we. Likewise wan, dizzy, from countless hours. Not having no events? In dark

---

♥Consider the precedents: in the 70s Denys Arcand film *Gina*, a drunk out cold in a snow bank gets sucked up in a snow blower, his bloody essence shooting high in scarlet arc against the night sky. Rumour has it that even now, occasionally, in winter, a homeless, or elder, citizen nearly similarly sucked up + ground to mush. Having slipped + fallen, having sunk slowly into the white bed under, unable to get up. Once, even, a toddler.

end of railway-flat Room. Stepping out + boarding #100 West. Métro Crémazie, direction Ikea. A pair of matching chicks. People were happier then. Having climbed th' artist-designed baroque-tiled triple double quadruple winding metro Cremazie steps. Having dropped our long-expired transfers into ticket receptacle. Having murmured th' traditional merci. Merci! To giant bearded-not-minding-cause-wanting-to-project-progressive chauffeur. Proceeding in two, three, four, different rhythms. To back horizontal bench. Nodding aflush, in idling diesel-fuel heat. When you, X, you impercipient carper from ailleurs. Hating not going to Ikea fast in a car. Whinnying too loud in English. Notwithstanding everyone on bus #100 en principe 100 percent French: —*How come queers in this place, this city Montréal, Québec. Supposedly so sexy, so risqué! Never seen smooching in public!* I/R refraining — which was probably advisable — from replying. That all things considered. Was it not hypocritical to be implying one more avant than the next? When wanting to go to Ikea in polluting private vehicle? For sole reason of individual comfort? Instead, turning other cheek. Direction: vieille madame on front reserved-for-handicapped seat. Herself, serendipitously cackling: —*Garde-moi ça: un nain.* Re: ~~dwarf~~ little person entering folding bus doors. Himself, instead of putting traditional expired transfer in receptacle. Standing. On balls of tiny feet. Reaching up up. And kissing bearded giant at wheel. Kissing. Kissing. Tiny tongue, flickering in + out of big hairy chauffeur's mouth. Small behind in nice-fitting jeans. Arched a very long time.

X, I was getting hot.

Wanting freedom

~~Th' freedom I looking for all—~~

Wanting le Palais des Nains♥ back where it was, Rachel East. Th' day you, my pseudo-Olympian. Having decided to be schussing. Schussing on back. Down dark inside stairs. And through open door. As if skiing on a glacier. Climbing up + schussing down on back again. With rapidly bruising folded-back knee. Simultaneously blast-pheming so loud. In English + other indecipherable vernaculars. French girl, leaning, straight-backed out window, laughing. Laughing, in bright autumn air. At I/R sneaking, sheepish, out of Settler-Nun court. Following

---

♥ As usual, we have to rely on the tabloids. Hence the *Journal*, when the little-people museum closing, proudly featuring shots of so-called Count + Countess Nichol. At home with their minuscule household accoutrements, in their 'palace' which from the 1920s was a museum of everyday life of local little people. Naturally, closing in the socially homogenizing 70s. Spectators are never neutral.

pair of crumpled autumn leaves. Wearing deep in their veins th' storms of generations. Blowing o'er parc. Once an orchard + th' orchard was watered. Blowing past triplex with Turkish dome pointing into cloud. Which cloud in extenso shadowing stucco Mission of Santa Cruz. Decked in her fluorescents. O'er boul Saint [people dubbing th' crease]. Grotty with creaky bars. Also, fine smoked meat. Th' pair of crumpled leaves serendipitously now in wake of stunning female little person. Long hair, bangs. Painted lips glancing back over tight pantsuited shoulder. So things might turn out for th' best. Having drawn this a.m. wheel of fortune. Inscribed with four points of th' compass: Bull Eagle Sphinx. Entwined snake. Her tiny pumps swinging East, on diagonal. Toward modest brick-+-stone façade. Provided by Shale Pit Workers! from nearby quarries, ca. 1900. Entering ground-floor door of Palais des Nains. Where little Count + Countess Nichol, in memoriam of circus: perpetually on display. Life-size Count photo welcoming guests. Tux, chapeau huit-reflets. Every perfect shiny object. Tiny, blue velvet sofa on shiny parquet floor. Beds, piano, toilet. To scale. With lowered ceilings, so fairy-tale. Normal.

Th' Countess [little prince in tummy] serving tea…

*

In faded light of stairwell, now jade as a crypt. I/th' fly still flouncin' a smidgen. Round-'n'-round-come-thither. In dewy-wet [*does not th' lord help them who help themselves?*] tutu. Titillatin' back of old C-N's neck, who, like all in R intrigue, so long denied his fantasy that his chain of words unable to emerge. Senescently mistakin', via keyhole: light spot, executin' laconic shuffle on stucco Room wall. For his beloved half-breed danseur à claquettes, Double Jos. Dousse. In whose almond gaze he, Casse-Noisette, once upon a time ejectin'. With liberal smugness of youthful avant Parisian: —*Je t'aime pour qui tu es.*

Seven steps down, our études-policières assistant also exhibitin' some élan. Havin' set aside purple monitor for purpose of essayin' postures. And gestures almost liquid — *does not all beauty require proportion of strangeness?*--for ce soir's Ligéia audition.

1. Eyes: delightful, appalling.

2. —*I don't care what anyone says, that wig Stephane's wearing really belongs to me!*

3. Arms: graceful, shrouded in ruby, revealing their whiteness. Here

The stagiaire precipitously remembering reality, if denied, implying retribution. Dutifully cocking ear for any mimic rout or treble. Darkly winging from under Room door. Where R corpus delicti on bed. Eyes wide open, possibly affixed on shadow branches shape-shifting along wall into attendant court of characters: judge, defence attorney, prosecutor [were we not all fearing precisely that?] While light spot, bobbing back out 4999 Settler-Nun casement, crossing spats. And leaping chairlike onto bent ice-thickened branch. But —

What is a ghost?

A flickering of memory?

No. A ~~ventriloquist~~ baby's high decibels. From parked car outside Bleue Nuit Tavern door. Just as I/R exiting Palais des Nains. Scoping, in car parked opposite, terror on a little sister's locked-in face. Leaning toward baby, over front vinyl car seat. Being responsible for keeping baby quiet — + okay. Continuing down walk, past open bar door. Where females dancing, knees in beery crotches. Splicing nerve ends of shattered men. I/R not ready for similarly soothing your, X, my tender's, terrible requitals, e.g., by no longer mentioning your own um doe-eyed infidelities. Therefore. IF! On opening middle gallery door, finding you inert. Due to glissading once too often on back down Triplex inner stairs. I/R surely kneeling on floor + placing fingers about your ivory throat. For spoiling our ... day.

Her Little Shelf a Cemetery

In now-total railway-flat black — resurgent thermal humming + cracking of iron-art-nouveau-hot-water radiator. Recipe for nostalgia cast ca. 1900 under Mayor Léonidas Villeneuve. Himself lumber scion of well-off Terrebonne farmer cum land speculator. Whose rosy luteinizing hormones driving force of North-South railway. Likewise all church + school construction. Sloped entrepreneurial shoulders, goateed chin, pate, providentially charging. Acuiting. Promoting: was not new Saint-Louis-du-Mile-End a paradise for families? Its thickets of stone + brick façades burgeoning along rues Settler-Nun, etc. Hélas, any citizen of this place, haplessly strolling out at night. Stumbling into unlit plumbing or cellar excavations —'*Shu fiche it to shay*: a painful sobering up. Mercifully, the town decreeing crossing planks for pedestrians. Meaning countless builders trundling up boul Saint. To Villeneuve's own lumber establishment, corner Good-Hunting. Purchasing snowy new-sawed lengths unequivocally exhaling hopeful forest odour, sticky with chewy resin. On little ridge overlooking new North terminus for Villeneuve's majority-owned Train du Nord railway, which ridge offering crow's-eye view of mushrooming gravel triplex roofs. Fanning South, direction Settler-Nun, where, this day of our lord,

November 6, 2003, pair of eyes, long + narrow, in dark end of Room, fixed on light spot leaping from glistening chairlike branch, back, via window, onto black mirrored mantel [Christmas-tree lights around]. With crumpled letter on it.

Dear Grandpa,

I/your granddaughter ~~am a liar~~ wanted to be authentic. After, I mean, just before the future. [And the future tale within, which is the realm of the ancestors. Beautifully turned out — a Sunday when one is gathered, photographed to be remembered. Adults smiling too wide.]

After wanting to be authentic, I/Rosine the liar relocating in 'je-me-souviens' part of continent. Deciding veritable alienation, + not failure to be of undisputed origin, the stuff of any novel. Albeit, pretending to Agathe, Boubou, Notebook, that, following the encounter with Untel♥

♥Untel? Ha! As old Gertrude Stein saying: If you're lost, return to beginning. Where our story first encountering, precisely, said Frère Untel [Brother Language], local cleric famous for aligning good French with well-being in his public letters: *Et comme je leur disais qu 'ils ne parlaient ni le français ni l'anglais, mais une langue bâtarde, un élève me répondit: 'On est fondateur d'une nouvelle langue.'* Even a little girl from the West, arriving in Notown [the East] knowing, on hearing the expression *famme t'y yelle*, to shut her trap.

152

['little conflagrations ... flaring up in the dark like lightning in a film noir'], I could never be the same. Some light, as I spoke, settling over tips of glasses + hairdos in East-end bar, where fitting in pretty well. With French learned in school in Notown [the East]. Jamais in Haeckville [the West]. True, more learned outside from Véro André Thérèse Françoise. Our principal, a lezzie, being chiefly enamoured of Latin. No one teaching anything ~~Algonquian~~.

Grandpa, can you see what a li—???

Still, today, looking out casement. Rain fell on sidewalk. Plink. Plink. Conjuring reading Catullus, for school, at Notown kitchen table. When Veeera extending skinny arm over checkered plastic tablecloth. And wiggling finger under brother Jos.'s nose. For saying you, Grandpa, speaking ~~Indian~~ Cree to Great-Grandma Dousse.

Grandpa, at her funeral, you said to Reeef:
    —*I want to thank you for marryin' Veeera, she could be a real bitch.*
    Then sotto voce to your former little fis':
    —*You killed her with your wildness.*
    I/Rosine. In interest of preserving copasetic Dousse family image. Hopping early flight back East. Grey front-

button skirt flapping open to knees. Nice pair of boots. Hoping to be ~~happy~~ famous. In so-called French part of continent. When Reeef unexpectedly marrying blonde lady from Europe, so back West again. Erroneously forgetting to pack slip for wearing under see-thru dress at wedding. —*Was Veeera*, I asking Reeef, over-loudly at reception [heart beating madly]. *Ever saying she Indigenous?* Silence a minute. His curly lashes dropping over spotted Celtic eyes, Reeef half-bowing in way of gentleman [but not quite officer] soldier: —*I don't think she knew.*♥ —*Any-way, adding Reeef. Aneewayee. It didn't bother me.*

Grandpa, the other day on #55 North [called the Bus of Defeat by a prof from McGill]. I/R, stuck to vinyl slow-bus seat, in sick November heat. Scrutinizing tired working faces. For [as is my wont] Aboriginal traces. The spike from brownie, bread, honey, midday wine. Causing sleep-insects in veins. Pores slack, open, osmosing all the ketone-y odours

---

♥ But since public discourse disseminates like billboards [i.e subliminally], let's hear, on the subject, the Dominion Province of Alberta's 1936 Royal Commission, investigating the conditions of 'half-breed' people: 'The half-breed … must either change his (Indian) mode of life to conform with that of the white inhabitants or he must gradually disappear. This is a hard alternative. Considerations of humanity and justice forbid that we should calmly or indifferently contemplate the latter …'

+ molecules, rising from all the exhausted flesh of all the workday people. Dipping no longer vertical on horizontal benches as conveyance slipping down under Good-Hunting overpass. Exiting immediately in low-bricked flat-sky quarter. Beyond spotty window, arched map of Italia, shaped like cocktail shoe. When I/R noting caramel-skinned woman across bus aisle. Smiling familiarly. Her skinny little daughter's face beside. Collapsing abruptly on Mama's shoulder. Into carved wood lines of the supremely exhausted. Balding wrestler-type beside turning huge torso scornfully away. Direction, Afro tot perched two rows back. On Mama's knee. Couettes. Crinolines. Dimples. —*THERE! Un vrai bébé là-là.* The guy [rose tattoo on arm], high-voiced, insinuating: —*Hé toé-là.* He's clapping chunky palms to get Afro tot's attention. —*Hé, tu connais ce jeu? Ta poupée veut jouer!* His voice thickening from simpery-mousy to baritone of 'rat.' Tot's maman: embarrassed. Other eyes around, not necessarily blue, lowering resentful. And though I/R wanting to be 'amber chick' to the rescue. Turning toward sun setting on brocade settees in storefront windows. Beyond Église-Sacré-Coeur-de-Saint-Jacques condos. Caffè Internationale. Bar Italia, etc. —*Eh toé-là*, iterating guy. *Veux-tu jouer avec moi?* I/R staring out. Remarkable how setting sky. Persisting in stomach.

Grandpa, in number of dreams lately. I'm in rural bus station. On prairies. Usual dust. Faded signs. Unable to recall phone nos. of men in the family. The line between faded + amber likewise unfortunately delible to Indigenous guy muttering sarcastically beside: —*Looks like a white woman. Talks like a white woman. Smells like, uh. . .* Which 'uh' rendering I/Rosine elated. Who sometimes also finding unpleasant the clatchy acidy smell rising off skin of Caucasians. Therefore regretting not carrying in wallet the photo of Veeera. Sad ancient eyes. Rez-school bowl haircut.♥ Bare four-year-old shoulders. Which photo now hanging on railway-flat stucco wall. In case Agathe or Notebook or anyone turning up some intemperate winter day. Snow + traffic animating exterior. All so integral.

Grandpa, did you ever get the postcard, signed Rosine in New York? Sunset on telephone building filling whole city

---

♥Consider the genealogy of the lie — + the lie of genealogy. Say, that bowl haircut on little Veeera's photo recalling, for some of Rosie's generation — suddenly interested in 'remembering' — the shorn braids of Indigenous residential-school children. But Veeera, raised as white, would not have shared the fate of even many mixed-race children on the fringes of white communities. Which children [dixit our aforementioned Royal Commission], were averse to going to school because 'ridiculed and humiliated by the white children.' And what to do with these 'half-breed' kids? Some of them, cautioned the commission, never go to school, yet often speak several languages. A priest warns: if these children are not schooled, they'll all be speaking Cree.

block. Toward whose pink plummet, I + very sophisticated US photog. friend one night strolling. Down hot summer street with smell of sulphur. Passing fortune teller's tiny scarlet storefront. Where, night before, after so-so Soho French supper: juicy chicken, Euro-style light-salted fries. Pencil-jeaned guy stepping up + offering enhanced sex in French for $$$. How I laughed, entering fortune teller's tiny alcove. Where woman, Latina, coughing, coughing. Taking my hand + crooning to ceiling: —*Never mind never mind. Under a future president all divided spirits healing. El choque de un alma altrapado el mundo del espiritu y el mundo de la tecnica a veces la deja entullada.* Which is why, Grandpa, I/R in repassing red alcove fortune-teller window with photog. Wondering what she meaning by 'spirit.' Could one more materially say 'marrow'? Spontaneously squinting eyes in red alcove windowpane reflection, to enhance strongest Aboriginal feature, I/R noticing fortune teller ce soir no longer, as usual, sitting in situ on little red sofa. Frightened-looking man, hair standing on end. Holding baby. —*The husband!* Saying newspaper vendor. *She had bad bad pneumonia. No insurance. Emergency ignoring.*

It's so easy to be murdered. Which is why in the streets of New York, better not to say too much. E.g., in quipping to photog. friend [squinting eyes again]: — *Do bones matter?*

She laughing: —*In your case, the give-away's all that Celtic hair.* Therefore I/R [mercifully] not recounting suspect story of dentist. In cross-shaped highrise. In middle of our Northern metropolis. Where one windy September day, opening faux-mahogany dentist door: office, pink + green, a Polynesian theme. Including receptionist. Settling in nice comfy dentist's chair. Vista of fluffy clouds scuttling back + forth between tops of buildings. When dentist [specializing in forensics for bodies pulled from river], declaring skull x-ray not Caucasian. —*What then?* I asking. —*Mongoloid,* he replying. —*Does that uh include Indian?* His 'could be' making me so happy. Yet simultaneously feeling shame. As if fascist lurking in room —

Grandpa: on subject of marrow. Was your paternal grandma Maria's lack of family name meaning she Indigenous? Was the Canuck Maria marrying somewhere au nord du Québec mixed? Or pure laine? Was your father the Shale Pit Worker! fleeing smallpox epidemy, really marrying an Ojibwa somewhere in Ontario? Whose offspring [you, Grandpa] marrying [but why only saying after she dying?], the *Métis,* Priscilla Daoust. Whose daughters, those oligeanous slide sisters. Often getting ready upstairs in Grandma's bedroom. For their Scot/Anglo/German husbands. Applying balms + camphor on-gu-ent to each other's pimples. I/R still recalling smell of faint lavender perfume. Covering something coming under potty commode door. Or from musky headless dollies in Victrola room. Opposite. Which olfactories rushing + cantilevering down banister. Encountering the Sunday meats. Bubbling in kitchen. Where Baby Rosie, sent to hang out with Grandma, sitting blissful on linoleum by wooden-toy drawer. Watching Grandma's ample breasts shaking shaking in loose cotton dress. With turning handle of ice-cream maker. Grandma, who rarely speaking. Unless scolding Johnsie the Irish char. For failing to wipe clean those spindle table legs.

Grandpa. Why Veeera saying you a Jew?♥ Why she saying 'Grandpa'? Instead of 'Papa'? Why, when selling diamonds, you reading teacups into bargain? Is it true your

---

♥ We might assert that diversionary tactics regarding origins were in anticipation of aversion, ventriloquized from the exterior, + internalized by the family along with the British-style Sunday roast. Grandpa in spats + vest, Grandma Prisc corseted under her rose moire gown, raising their defences against the widespread lack of purchase for half-breed businessmen. Hear, again, our dear Commission: 'The readiness with which the half-breed succumbed to the wiles and persuasions of speculators in parting with the scrip [small land grants to Métis, post-resistance] indicates his lack of business foresight ... '

own legendary person was featured in a Rocky Mountain novel? Tight silk purple-shirted cowgirl on cover upon your sleeping chest in hammock. Grandpa, did you really find one day, riding your beautiful Appaloosa, the entire railway payroll? Which payroll you honourably returning, mid local newspaper fanfare [the emptier the landscape, the grander the opportunities!]. Did you really ride bulls with Jesse James's brother? And dance la claquette in Montréal, Chicago, ultimately in Paris? How, when somethin'-not-right arrivin' [indistinct shadowy chronicles, with dotty photos of you in blizzard, very well-dressed, surreptitiously pushing wheelbarrow of 'borrowed' coal through dark Depression winter, which coal, you reluctantly revealing, for aiding freezing lady neighbour] —how you getting out of it all right? How surviving driving your jeep off a cliff? How surviving, at 80, falling snowsuited in icy mountain lake, so waterlogged they towing you to shore behind the boat? How flying, without getting robbed, all over continent with jewels in your purse [catching your death of cold in Florida]? Grandpa, for us you were the future [+ the future tale within]. Whose tale's omissions contributing to succeeding generations' inability to communicate with open-mindedness, understanding, steadfastness of principles, consequently, always putting up defence walls of near paranoia. To wit: your story of Great-Grandma at the ranch.

NOW [you always starting a story with 'now']: NOW. Quite a blizzard! Your Great-Grandma Dousse, looking out window. Unable to see a thing. Then an Indian [sic]. Standing very still. In door. Snow-covered blanket. Horse half-buried. In Cree, she offering him stew. After he eating, she asking: —*How is your wife?* —*Oh*, said he. *She's. Outside. On pony.* Would Great-Grandma herself, being 100 percent Indian, have said not 'an Indian' but 'a man.' Standing in door?

Ha! I saw a picture of Grandma Prisc. With Baby Dill, your favourite, on a cradleboard. So why you hating Veeera? Watching, in nice pleated shorts, polka-dot blouse, from a corner of the photo. Your brown hand offering baited hook to little albino cousin on gravel shore of idyllic river rushing forward, clear, happy. True, the bored tilt of Veeera's chin giving scene a certain cheeky angle. Did she press you to speak frankly, given that the ventriloquism of strangers requiring great deal of monitoring? Because the minute you let up, something bad happening.

The other day, Grandpa, I/Rosine on bed. Relaxed for a minute. Watching snowflakes beyond railway-flat casement. Falling, falling. Smell of traffic + doughnuts. Rising somewhere fresh in pot. Not les 'pets-de-nonnes,' shaped precisely like 'the farts of nuns.' We used to get. But those empty in middle. Like Grandma making. Whose lovely fresh odour recalling Veeera, expiring on divan. Tummy swollen from sugar + wheat. Very pale from refusing in summer to let tanning sun fall, even on back of little finger. Also retching if tongue contacting motherskin of milk. Dark-auburn hair, already dead to the touch, spread over intense velvet cushion. Hand-piquéed-by-Grandma: sprouting very substantial rose in middle, multi-layered + darker fuchsia deep between the petal creases, sinking into blackness of the fabric under. The house cracking under weight of snow + ice. On turquoise soccer-ball computer monitor by casement. Surprise invitation to dinner, suddenly last Saturday. Where, during a very nice salmon, little girl with clear strong features. French. Québécois. Greek. Indigenous. Also Caucasian-American ancestors. Laughing + saying

   —*Eeeeeeeengleeesh?*

Afterword

Our story exists, as it were, 'in its own right.' One exception to all freedom from 'the facts': certain grandfather tales, themselves rather 'tall,' were passed down the generations.

The map is likewise unreliable, and unstable. A new town appears on the prairies. Rivers get displaced. An orchard grows in a park. Montréal street and neighbour-hood names shift and stick between languages. The 'Shale Pit Workers!' were actually stone quarriers, but got mistranslated in a document unearthed by the author. The mistranslation seemed relevant. It seemed relevant as well to make them legendary.

People float between the real world and the world of the dead. For some, time does not matter. For some it matters terribly. The protagonist, Rosine, drifts between her parts: the woman in the Room, the fly on the wall, and the Bottom Historian, ever in denial about her secret desire for omniscience.

Acknowledgements

The late Robert K. Martin offered gracious support and inspiration. Many thanks to Mile-End Historian Susan Bronson, to Karen Herland, Robert Schwartzwald, Bruce Russell, Kathryn Harvey, Anna Isacsson, Roger des Roches, Bill Kennedy, Rachel Levitsky [and the Belladonna Elders' Series], Kate Eichhorn. And to my family. Thanks to the amazing writers of the Ogamas Brandon Aboriginal Literary Festival.

This work has benefitted from several grants and residencies, including the Canada Council, le Conseil des arts et des lettres du Québec, Université de Montréal, the Banff Centre, Millay Colony, Virginia Centre for the Creative Arts, St. Norbert Arts Centre.

The character MacBeth cites passages, sometimes adapted, from the Shakespearean playwright of the same [but spelt differently] name. The description of the alleys during the smallpox epidemy is indebted to Micheal Bliss's seminal *Plague*. Other authors who have stepped into this tale include Mordecai Richler, Edgar Allen Poe, Alfred Hitchcock, Viktor Shklovsky, Water Benjamin, William Burroughs, Tomson Highway, Maria Torok and Nicholas Abraham, Hölderlin, Virgil and Maya Angelou.

Thanks, finally, to Stephen Motika.

Gail Scott

The Obituary is Gail Scott's fourth novel. Her prose experiments can also be found in the novels *My Paris*, *Main Brides* and *Heroine*, as well as essays, stories, manifestoes and collaborations with Nicole Brossard et al (*La théorie, un dimanche*), and Robert Glück, Camille Roy, and Mary Burger (*Biting the Error*). She teaches Creative Writing at Université de Montréal.

Originally published in Canada by Coach House Books, Toronto, in 2010.

ISBN: 978-1-937658-03-8

Design and typesetting by HR Hegnauer
Text set in Adobe Caslon Pro
Cover by Helen Mirra
Triplex sketch on page 22 by Philippe C. Lefebvre

Cataloging-in-publication data is available
From the Library of Congress

Distributed by University Press of New England
One Court Street
Lebanon, NH 03766
www.upne.com

Nightboat Books
Callicoon, New York
www.nightboat.org

Nightboat Books

Nightboat Books, a nonprofit organization, seeks to develop audiences for writers whose work resists convention and transcends boundaries. We publish books rich with poignancy, intelligence, and risk. Please visit our website, www.nightboat.org, to learn about our titles and how you can support our future publications.

This book has been made possible, in part, by a grant from the New York State Council on the Arts Literature Program.

State of the Arts

NYSCA